# Sterling Road Blues

MAY 2010

# Ruth Perkinson

Bella
BOOKS
2010

Bella Books, Inc.
P.O. Box 10543
Tallahassee, FL 32302

Printed in the United States of America on acid-free paper
First Edition

Editor: Katherine V. Forrest
Cover Designer: Linda Callaghan

ISBN 10: 1-59493-187-9
ISBN 13:978-1-59493-187-1

## The Lake Isle of Innisfree

*by William Butler Yeats*

*I will arise and go now, and go to Innisfree, And a small cabin build there, of clay and wattles made: Nine bean-rows will I have there, a hive for the honey-bee, And live alone in the bee-loud glade.*

*And I shall have some peace there, for peace comes dropping slow, Dropping from the veils of the morning to where the cricket sings; There midnight's all a glimmer, and noon a purple glow, And evening full of the linnet's wings.*

*I will arise and go now, for always night and day I hear lake water lapping with low sounds by the shore; While I stand on the roadway, or on the pavements grey, I hear it in the deep heart's core.*

*For Mom, Dad, Mary Kathryn and Page.*

*Also, for my dog, River, and the Virginia Home.*

# Acknowledgments

Books are difficult labors of love. For this one, I'd like to thank my family and my publisher and my editor for staying behind me and backing me all the way.

My mother continues to teach me about grace and love and what it takes to keep a family together. The lessons are still there and each and everyday I'm honored to be her daughter. She is a true role model of how a human being should be. Without her and my loving sister this book would not be.

All my love to Heather Campbell who reads the pages and nudges me in the right spots. You're a beautiful, gifted woman. I regard you as you should be regarded.

Katherine Forrest – you are a charm. You are a charm for writers and have given this era of writing an indelible soul that will know no time. I don't know much, but this I know for sure. Thank you for your edits and your uncanny ability to understand me and my quirks better than me.

Linda Hill – thank you for number four and continuing to make my dreams come true.

Special thanks go to Dyana Mason, Ryan Burgess, and Terri Nelson. All of these special women have given me their time and their knowledge to help this book along.

Finally, I'd like to acknowledge special needs people of all walks of life – whether it is a physical or mental incapacity. These people have made my life rich and full and better than I ever thought it could be. Handicapped people are the true heroes of this world.

## About the Author

Ruth Perkinson lives in Richmond, Virginia with her dog, River. She is the author of Vera's Still Point, Piper's Someday, and Breaking Spirit Bridge. She is currently working on her fifth novel. You can read more about her at www.ruthperkinson.net.

# Chapter 1

The year the first African-American president took the hot seat in the oval office, exactly two-and-a-half hours south of the nation's Capitol, a young twenty-one-year-old Down Syndrome girl graduated with honors from rural Sterling Road High School. Equally impressive feats.

However, Elizabeth Cichetti did not understand politics or the grave state of the economy. She was, in the words of her teenage contemporaries, too stupid, too retarded. She understood recess, lunch, basketball, the names of critical teachers and hugs: all honorable in the eyes of her special ed teacher, Ms. Audra Malone.

On the June day Elizabeth Cichetti graduated, she wore a white oxford button-down shirt, khaki pants that were a size too big because she liked to bust-a-sag. Adorning her feet were her blue basketball sneakers, the laces double-knotted, and on her wrist was an orange band that had *UVA Women's Basketball* imprinted on it. In her pocket was a green flippy frog, which when you wound it up, it rifled backwards and landed on its webbed feet. It mesmerized both her and the EMR mute she was in love with, Melissa Fortunata, for hours.

My fifth period had called them both r-e-e-e-tards for some time before a nervous male Delegate from the state General Assembly came walking into our cafeteria to eat fudgies and ask me and Audra Malone questions about lobby day and Gay-Straight Alliance's legal status in historically one of the reddest states in the country and the concept of marriage, errr, gay marriage, for special populations.

I called her Cichetti and most people and students by their last names. An old habit I'd picked up playing collegiate basketball and softball a million years ago.

"It's for luck, Mith Tomlinthon," Cichetti said, pointing to her wristband and hugging my leg.

"Luck is good. You're going to need it," I said back, crossed my eyes at her and stuck my tongue out then squeezed her shoulder.

Cichetti giggled. "Wher's yurs?" she asked, choking in her swollen tongue, peering down and holding my hand and wrist up in dismay. Then she felt around in my pocket to see if I had a flippy frog in mine. Her mouth was agape. She rubbed her nose, then wiped the remnants on her shirt and returned her gaze to my wrist then back up to me. Elizabeth Cichetti—still looking at me like I was the demigod I knew I wasn't. Her dark, rich almond eyes, intense and feeling and wondering and she didn't even know she was doing it.

I shifted my black robe and gold and white alma mater colors and scanned the packed bleachers on the football field of the high school. There were blue ribbons everywhere and the June air was filled with hope, hairspray and humidity. "I left it on my dresser at home, Cichetti girl."

"Why are you callin' me that Mith Tomlinthon?"

"Cuz you're driving me crazy!"

2

"Mith Tomlinthon, you are crazy." She looked at my wrist again, then looked at me.

We had all been a little crazy this year.

The band began and Elizabeth's special ed. teacher, Audra Malone, came to get her for the lineup. The blue and orange colors of her UVA alma mater were draped on her, making her look hot, languid and tired. But Malone was stiff as starch underneath it all and had been all year. Curiously, she always clenched her teeth as if this would intensify her thoughts or her feelings or her situation, the muscles in her cheek sticking out. It amused me. She amused me. Her black loafers were dusty from the track and her pear-shaped body was hidden beneath her robe. Beyond her, the football field was lined with a rickety stage that held the administration already positioned for the ceremony. Rusted folding chairs were lined up for the students in the middle and the faculty seats were off to the right of the students. I could smell the freshly cut grass through the drugstore perfume of the seniors milling about in their black robes and mortar boards, all looking excited and lost at the same time, many scanning the crowd in search of fat Uncle Ralph or Nanny Mable. Malone looked back at what I was looking at and then pointed at her watch and then slowly reached for Cichetti's hand, which still held my wrist, and with precision and a weird solemnity took hers from mine.

"Hey, Ms. Tomlinson? May I borrow Elizabeth and get her in line?" Malone asked.

"Malone, you can do anything you want with this young girl, she's earned it, you think?"

I said this and then flipped my colors around and walked over to take my position with the faculty lineup. We were about to march into the thirty-second annual Sterling Road High School graduation and I longed for a top-shelf margarita.

The bleachers sagged in the center from the heaviness of a thousand or so families and friends and underclassmen, half of whom were nose down texting their friends sitting three rows behind them. All getting carpal tunnel of the thumbs.

I gazed at Malone and Cichetti. Malone's auburn hair was thick with the wetness from the humid air. Her gait slowed to stay with Cichetti whose appearance was like any person with Down Syndrome appeared: almond shape to the eyes caused by having weaker eyelids; limbs shorter than normal and her tongue stuck out some; and, her hair was short and cut in a bowl shape and she talked with a lisp. Cichetti loved to talk and giggle and smile and be silly. Traits I assigned to the syndrome. Traits I wanted to assign to most everyone.

She and Malone walked over to some of the other special ed. students who were finding their footing and finding their places in line. When Cichetti caught sight of her girlfriend, Melissa Fortunata (or Fort as she called her) in the stands, she yelled, "Hey, Fort!" and waved with both hands in loving fury. I turned my sights to Fortunata, who sat with two volunteers from the Charlottesville Home and with River, Malone's therapy dog. Melissa Fortunata would not be graduating from Sterling Road High School along with the other special ed. students because of events beyond her control: like parents and asshole kids. Her "ousting" from the school had been filled with hatred, redneck boys and parents paralyzed in poverty and shame.

In glee, Fortunata waved back at her girlfriend and patted River, a dark shepherd-mix, on the head at the same time. Fortunata's face was round, almost swollen, and her ears stuck out in an elfish way. Her heaviness lay thick on her bones as she loved to eat just like Cichetti. One eye was slower than the other and she could only say about ten words. And, if she did speak, it was to Cichetti, Malone and the dog. Fortunata did not have Down Syndrome. She was educably mentally retarded and most called her a dumb mute.

Fort had become so accustomed to Malone's dog that she accompanied her almost everywhere, including the bathroom. The bathroom was the scariest place for Fort. But, if River went with her, then she could handle it.

I rolled my eyes and craned my neck to look up at the sky. What a year!

Cichetti yelled at Fort again, and the crowd started to become unusually quiet. The band struck up again and the faculty line began to move with a little pomp and a little circumstance, me included.

I hadn't had a drink in three months.

Sterling Road High School was centered in the middle of Route 163 in Crozet, Virginia and had been sitting on its solid brick foundation for more than sixty years, named after the road it situated itself on. Sterling Road was famous for Colonel Hickock Sterling who fought alongside J.E.B. Stuart in the 37th Cavalry of Virginia. Sterling was famous for his bravery in getting J.E.B. Stuart to Gettysburg during the most critical hours of Robert E. Lee's campaign. Sterling was killed by taking a bullet that was surely on its way to crippling the gallant Stuart who would later die after a mortal wound at the battle of Yellow Tavern near Richmond. When someone displayed the kind of gallantry that Sterling showed, usually a road or a marker or a river or stream was the honorary way to commemorate them.

The high school itself was nestled in the bucolic Blue Ridge Mountains; therefore, we were called the Blue Ridge Mountain Dogs or just the Blues for short. It ran a bit contrary to the rebel gray we should have been but no one seemed to care.

Behind the school were the football fields and corresponding baseball and softball fields. Nearer to the school was the soccer field where Malone took her exceptional ed students with a place to sit on a bench where a brook filled with large and small stones and ran north toward Charlottesville, Virginia—only thirty minutes from where our school drooped in the middle of nowhere.

Just eight months earlier in the school's yellowed and cracked concrete administration building at the front of Sterling Road High School, Elizabeth Cichetti had swirled around in her pretend roller-coaster seat next to the overly thin attendance secretary, Peggy Schindler. Peggy had OCD, or so I speculated, as everything was in a neat stack and arranged in colored file folders in prim, proper and precise ways. Everything had a label and her stapler, tape and pen cup were arranged like soldiers next to her phone and message pad. The school's announcement system with its colored buttons and silvery microphone was antiquated, but budgets are budgets and this dinosaur would have to last.

With her swollen tongue half-protruding from her mouth, the cause of her on-again, off-again lisp, Cichetti waited to read the cafeteria's menu for the day. She had gotten the job as the head-menu-reader-in-charge after she begged for the fifteen billionth time for her special ed. teacher, Malone, to let her. Cichetti usually asked for what she wanted between fourteen and fifteen billion times. Finally, exasperated and sick of seeing her flip her frog on her desk, Malone gave in. "You can do it Elizabeth as long as Mrs. Schindler is okay with it." Later, Malone had asked her by the faculty bulletin board, a hot spot for teacher congregators, and Schindler pushed up her thick reading glasses and with pursed lips said, "No problem."

That particular day, it unveiled as it normally did. I thumbed through my faculty mail at our mailboxes just eight feet or so from Schindler's desk: flier, coupon and a lot more nothing. God had performed divine intervention this particular year and I did not have a first-period class. So, I watched Elizabeth every day until this fated day in late October. She would swivel around, flip her frog, and then sidle up next to Peggy and wait for Peggy to do the usual: cancel a ball game; announce a new hallway monitoring procedure; give it up for the athlete-of-the week; give out times and dates for cheerleading practice as well as which club was meeting when. At the end of Peggy's announcements, she would hand over the mic to Cichetti. The mic was her holy piece of equipment, the cell phone she never got, her link to the world, at least the world of SRHS—and she would always say it with her lisp like this:

"Good morning Th-terling Road High Th-chool,

Thith ith Elizabeth Cichetti and hereth what the cafeteria ith having for lunch today:

6

Th-paghetti with meatballs, th-alad, fruit cup and fudgie-th. Goodbye for today, Th-terling Road High Th-chool."

The menu changed each day but her opener and closer stayed the same: "Good morning SRHS and goodbye for today, SRHS." She became an instant hit and the cafeteria's longstanding poor relationship with making any money at all seemed to have been given an economic boost because Cichetti had become its th-pokesperthon. She was the miracle on the microphone and her own physical and mental anomaly was mitigated by her charismatic voice, lisp and all.

She high-fived Peggy Schindler, and then she came up to me and did the same. *Smack*. She showed me her bracelet and asked me where mine was. I shrugged. Embracing my runner's leg, she peered up. At five-eleven, I had to always look down as Cichetti's head hit me in between my breastbone. My hands automatically reached for the top of her head and I muffed her silky rich hair then held her cheeks in my hands momentarily.

Three teachers walked by us without notice and I congratulated Cichetti on her announcing. "You're a pro at that microphone, Cichetti. What a voice you have!"

She released my leg and put her hands in the air as if she'd scored a touchdown. "Can I go shoot baskets, Mith Tomlinthon?" she asked. This is what she asked me fifteen billion times a day.

"Go to class, Cichetti. Ms. Malone has some good stuff going on today." I put my hands through my hair, feeling hung over from the six beers on an empty stomach from the night before. My head was cobwebby and my gut felt hollow.

"I can see Fortunata!" she yelled and I saw Principal Snodgrass lean to look through his office door. "Fort, Fort, Fort!" And she strolled through the front doors of the front office to walk down the outside corridor to the special ed. wing. Through the windowpane of the front office, with the blinds opened, you could hear Cichetti stomp away and the muffled words of Fort, Fort, Fort, trail away in the air as the October leaves swirled and whirred in eddies as the front door slammed shut.

Once again, I smoothed over my own short-cropped hair and

wiped the oily mascara from underneath my eyelids as I turned to walk to my classroom to prepare for the day. Two steps and I could still hear Cichetti. Internally giggling, I felt a sudden and proud shift in myself for having hired Cichetti to be my basketball manager. For three straight years, Malone, my best friend and confidant, had asked me to have Cichetti on the team. I gave in during her senior year and said she could be part of the team as manager. Malone told Cichetti and she didn't seem to understand the difference between manager and player. All was well.

Ole Cichetti girl. She made no sense. Going to see Fort.

I really didn't care.

Momentarily, I was caught staring at the faculty bulletin board, but my mind was misty and floating elsewhere. Suddenly, in the middle of my gape, I became drunk with a sort of orgiastic wine that soaked into my bones so deep I thought I might stop breathing. I didn't want to think of her. Jesus, not now. Not at school. My recent maligned love affair with number twenty or twenty-five or eighty-six. I couldn't keep up with my promiscuity. Victoria Simbleton, who had recently dumped me via e-mail, had intoxicated me to the core and made me drunk with sex like I'd never been drunk before. We had made love six or seven times a day and I walked bowlegged to get beer while my legs throbbed from what just was and throbbed in anticipation as to what was to come next. Elixir.

I tried to break from staring at the bulletin board by glancing over at Schindler. She was busying herself at her computer and sitting so ergonomically correct it almost made me laugh.

After three sex-filled months, Simbleton, now renamed Simpleton, had just left me heartbroken and now I, ironically, was teaching my English classes how to write epitaphs for Halloween. Death. Death of relationships. Death of hope. I was left to shake out my emotions over birth dates and death dates of my suddenly famous yet deceased students as I handed out the assignment. I gave them examples of how Poe might have written his epitaph or perhaps Emily Dickinson or even Henry David Thoreau. Poe might be dark and ominous; Dickinson full of clipped brevity; and Thoreau looking for some meaning in the leaves or bark. I read from Spoon River Anthology and then just wanted to die from having been my own stupid ass. My epitaph: I don't care because I'm a stupid ass. How can someone have sex that often and have a committed relationship? I had fallen in love with the sex. Always my Achilles heel.

I explained epitaphs through the veil of Victoria Simpleton (still parked in my brain) through the first classes of my day and then went to the dreaded lunch duty to keep students from cutting in line and killing each other over chicken nuggets, french fries and the entrée of the day: spaghetti.

From my classroom, the cafeteria was a fair distance away in the back near the soccer field. Upon arrival, one needed earplugs from the yelling and the maelstrom of wiggers, punks, athletes, cheerleaders, rednecks, hip-hop brothas and sistahs and the clandestine band groupies, the secret outsiders. The lunch line wrapped around in the middle and the students looked like cattle being herded through the doors of the lunch line where the one-hundred-year-old cafeteria workers looked simultaneously hollow, tired and scared. Food was thrown onto plates and no eye contact was made. Just what do you want and hurry the hell up. Next. Everyone had an area, a group, and a habit of sitting in the same place. Teachers were no different.

I had lunch duty with Cichetti's teacher and my best friend—the other gay member of the faculty: Audra Malone. I estimated she'd had sex four times in her life and three of them had been with herself.

Still, she was on my team and I was glad of it.

# Chapter 2

When I walked into the cafeteria later that morning after teaching epitaphs, Malone saw my face and bought me an Eskimo Pie. She was dressed in her usual style: casual brown loafers, dark velvet pants and a loose navy cashmere sweater that had a pumpkin pin on it. We had been good friends since our college days: she at UVA and me at Virginia Tech. We had met at a gay bar in Roanoke, Virginia and gotten drunk over politics and poontang. She could outtalk me on politics but not on the pootie. "Shut up on the pootie," she said to me then. I told her that I would not shut up on the pootie. She said she would not shut up on the politics. We instantly liked each other. Neither one of us could shut our respective pieholes about what was gravely important in our small lives.

"You look like you should put a sheet over your head. Here." She handed me the pie. "What's wrong with you? Your hair is sticking out." She smoothed it over. "And your eyes look like they haven't slept since the nineteenth century. You look dumpy and destitute. Your hair looks blacker than black. Button your shirt up one."

"Nice alliteration and your use of similes makes me hot. Sexwich Simpleton broke up with me via e-mail. I drank six beers last night before I attempted suicide by holding my breath," I said bluntly, buttoning my black corduroy shirt. "Does sugar help? I'm despondent, desolate and dense."

"Yes to dense and yes to sugar. Sometimes I go into the refrigerator at home and get some Reddi-wip and turn it upside down in my mouth for a good ten seconds. Try it over the beer. Usually does the trick. Dare I ask the reason for the breakup?" Malone turned over her papers and put her hands through her thick auburn hair. She was short, squatty and frumpy and her nose jutted out cleanly over her thin upper lip like a hook but mushed in like she was constantly pressed up to a pane of glass. Butch but cute. Her shoulders were square and she was short but not small. She checked the vicinity to see if our gay coast was clear.

"We never dated." I licked the vanilla ice cream and sighed. Three kids from my fifth period were arguing over something but I turned my head and ignored it. I couldn't deal. I scooted my plastic chair in closer to the folding brown table and extended my lanky legs. "These kids are never going to get along." I snuck a peek at the special ed. table. "But, what do I care." Another lick and all I could think about was me, me, me. My dark-headed ego had surfaced again. Now, I couldn't breathe. Bloody Mary suicide later.

Malone threw her head back in complete giggledom. "Carrie Tomlinson! You never dated? Did you even get her last name and if she was free of any communicable diseases before the sexcapades started?"

"Shut it up, Malone. I asked her about diseases."

"Between breaths or after you became Muffy the diver?" She crunched a french fry and squirted ketchup all over her paper plate, her right finger was adorned with a fake red-silver ring she never took off except to wash my dishes when she was at my house.

"Okay. Is this comic routine going to continue? We're writing epitaphs in my classes. Need me to do yours?"

"No, but you may need to do one for your crotch. 'Licker she did, done lickered out.'"

I paused and she saw that she had stung me for a moment. But, I didn't care.

I ate the end of my Eskimo Pie. "Subject change before the floodgates open and you have to medevac me to the clinic for tissue supplies."

"Carrie, here's a napkin. Sorry. Did you see Elizabeth Cichetti after basketball practice yesterday?" Malone ate with a precarious slowness, chewing every bit as if she prayed on it.

"Are you changing the subject? Even though I'm despondent? Even though I am a victim of unrequited love?"

"Shut up, Shakespeare. Yes. Seems like you could use something besides yourself to talk about. You're all you talk about. Noticed?" She patted me on the back. "You know I'm here, don't you. Me. Malone?" She laughed at this. "What number is this one?"

"What number are you on? What's your name?" For a second, my trouble with Simpleton slowed and I was glad to be in hell with Malone. Modern day school cafeterias were like Dante's *Inferno* but worse. Schools in general were worse.

Tulio Grayson, one of my fifth period rap heads, got up and started to flirt with three black girls from my third-period class at the table behind them. Then Jack Ignatio the redneck farm boy joined him. The girls seemed edgy but I ignored it. Three of my basketball players waved at me when they emptied their trays into the trashcan. I waved back.

"Okay, I agree. This despondency of mine really has to go. It's just that the me in me doesn't want to quit. So, what's going on with Cichetti? I did lose her for a while after practice yesterday. But, then again, I lose her all the time. I don't know how you do it with teaching special ed. kids all the time. Does God dole you guys out more in the patience department? It would drive me nuts. She drives me nuts."

"Do you want to hear the story or do you want to pontificate. Cuz this pontification is really boring me."

"Go ahead." I noticed the clock. We only had a few minutes left.

"Anyway—are you listening?"

"Yes, I was just noticing the clock."

"Okay. So, I'm coming out of lazy Larry's lab class with Dean Dickhead Snodgrass because Billie Sprinkle has tried to burn his lab partner with the Bunson burner."

"How do you burn someone with a Bunson burner?"

"Am I boring you with the fact that you lost Elizabeth and I've bought you two Eskimo Pies and my narrative hook sucks cuz I lost you at the Bunson burners."

"Okay. I'll shut up. What do you know about narrative hooks anyway? What happened with Cichetti?" I finished off the pie and tossed it in the trash at the end of the food line. I yelled at Jack and Tulio to sit down but they ignored me. In my head I told them to fuck off, along with Simpleton. Students began to run back for dessert before the bell rang to signal the five-minute rush before fifth period began.

"So, listen to me…focus. She's out by the edge of the foyer to the gym and she's doing that thing with her mouth because we've had a bit of autumn shower. So, she's catching drops and guess who comes barreling around the corner like she's been shot out of one of lazy Larry's tornado funnels…you know the one…"

"I know. Keep going. Who comes around the corner?"

"Melissa Fortunata." She put her hands up and then down. Malone's shirt came out of her black pants and the top button on her shirt came undone underneath her sweater.

"Yeah. So what about Fortunata?" I reached over to button her shirt.

"Stop!" She brushed my hand away. "I can do that."

She fumbled nervously with her hands and got the button

secured. "Well. So, I'm standing there looking at the detention notice for Billie Sprinkle and hoping his mouth doesn't start with every expletive since he began learning words at five, when Fortunata starts doing her mouth the same way that Elizabeth is doing hers."

"Okay. I'm fading back into my misery. You've lost me. It must be time for another Eskimo Pie or maybe a fudgie, eh?"

"Carrie. Listen. Fortunata doesn't really do much mimicking and she can only say about ten words anyway and then the craziest thing happened."

"You dropped your pencil and Sprinkle picked it up because he was emoting." I smiled and cringed at the same time.

"Shut up. All of this is catharsis for you."

"Oh. Now you've got me with your vocabulary," I went to high-five her but she dissed me.

"Fortunata reached for Elizabeth's hand and they held hands." Malone glanced around like the hand-holding police might show up. I followed her glances as if I expected someone to show up too.

"Malone. It's okay if she holds her hand. What's wrong with that? Do we need to get the Gay-Straight Alliance on high alert to see if there may be some fallout with the neo-Nazi group or the badass hip-hop gang or the redneck football stars that Tulio and Jack belong to? They all have their own Harriet Tubman underground, you know? You know they will need someone to pick on and picking on a Down Syndrome and an EMR kid will just be their ticket to hell, their ticket to pride, their ticket to making their dicks bigger, their ticket to—"

"I just thought you might want to watch Elizabeth to make sure she keeps her knickers along the straight and narrow when I'm not around to do it for her. I'm just afraid some of the wrong kids will see them and it will cause bedlam."

"Elizabeth Cichetti is the one student who will either keep me teaching or send me to the nearest insane asylum," I said.

"Why's that?"

"Because—hey Jeremy pick that wrapper up!—because I'm

14

always losing her. I lose her at practice. Evidently, now she's holding hands with Melissa Fortunata, and I lose her at basketball games. Just last week when we were playing Nelson High, she shot baskets with the other team till I caught her doing it."

"Carrie, I do believe you have more worries than some diseased hottie from over in Stony Point. Get over her…as quickly as you can!" Malone got up.

"And get under who?"

"Yourself. I'll see you at the GSA meeting later, okay. Will you need more chocolate or do I need to go out for the cans of Reddi-wip?"

"I'll need a tourniquet for your mouth."

"Oooo. I'm so scared. Make sure you bring the meeting guidelines. This is our second meeting and I want to make sure we do the meetings with the right kind of propriety."

"Will you hold my hand?"

"Shut up."

After lunch, I had the toughest class of my day. Twenty-four boys and six girls. Most of the boys were athlete wannabes with long nylon sport shirts that hung down to their knees. The jeans were held up by wide stances and hands pulling up their jeans to their hips every six to eight seconds. All shoes were large, laces untied. Jack Ignatio was the ringleader of the bunch. He renamed himself Jack Doff on the second week of class and it was the first time I had sent a kid to the office in more than six years.

"What's wrong with renaming yourself Jack Doff, Ms. Tomlinson? Come on, you know you like it."

It was the 'you know you like it' part that sent him to the office. My face had turned blood red and Tulio Grayson pointed it out and laughed so hard he fell out of his desk.

"Tulio, you're next—"

"I'd be glad to be next." He licked his lips and then he was gone. Two down. I was down to twenty-eight kids.

"Anyone else?"

After the two incidents, I assigned them a poetry recitation project that any third grader could pass. But this class was dumber than you could imagine. No, it was unimaginable. The average IQ I think was just over one hundred, but most of them had done so much blotter or trash drugs that they had snorted their IQs up their nose and out their ass. I was stuck with them for the next one hundred and fifty-nine days of school. I put my hands on my face and felt my sunken eyes from too many nights of drinking. My skin was dry but my small French nose felt oily from too many fried foods and my thin lips were chapped. Oxymoron, oily chapped—slick and dry. I reached for my Chapstick and gave myself some relief. For a moment, I imagined Cichetti and Fortunata holding hands and catching raindrops with their mouths. Placing my hands on the back of my neck for support, I peered through my window and longed to be riding in my car down Sterling Road away from this place. My room was a prison cell.

Of the six girls, I did have some hope for Sherry Proffitt except that she was so large and wore Goth clothes only to hide her two-hundred-and-fifty-pound frame. She had not spoken since the first day of class when I asked her name and she mumbled it like it was a disease she didn't want anyone to know about. When she walked into the room, the boys laughed under their IQ-less breaths and sometimes I heard farm animal noises. I glared at who I thought had made the noise, but if you couldn't pinpoint it—you could not arrest the bastard making the comment and have his balls cinched in a tight sack. At least that's how I felt about it.

They knew I was gay. I was the girls' basketball coach for crying out loud. It came with the sport, much like softball and flag football. We didn't have flag football yet but some of the girls were kicking for the football team.

Jack Doff came back from the office the next day and told me he'd stick with cross-dressing and not name-changing.

This class was trouble.

But the trouble with me this year was that I didn't much care. Out of economic fear and stupidity, I'd already cashed out what was left of my retirement to garner some spending money to

16

pay for booze and nights out and basketball sweats for the girls whose parents couldn't afford them. I was stuck here.

Gay old times.

# Chapter 3

Before basketball practice and later that day, I was forced by Malone to attend the Gay-Straight Alliance or GSA meeting. Oy vay. In this place, an oxymoron. I was the moron. I just wanted to be down Sterling Road on my way home. No problems. No losing Elizabeth Cichetti. Nothing. A fifth period flown to someplace in the moonshine woods where they could all write epitaphs or recite the wisdom from their white-hooded forebears. I didn't care. I just wanted out of here. What a day. I needed alcohol and a chat with Susan. That would help the sting.

"Malone, did you bring the folders for the GSA kids?" I asked as we pulled up beside each other in the hallway on the west wing of school: 3:45 p.m. I noticed on a clock above room 442. Her loafers clacked on the floor and she looked tired from the day. Her shirt was untucked and I pulled on it to be silly.

"Yes, Ms. Tomlinson. I did. Are you going to run the meeting or am I?"

Clack, clack, clack she went down the hallway, stretching her arms in the air and making no eye contact. Two Asian students sat on the floor with papers spread in front of them.

"Are you kidding. I barely was willing to sign up for this gig. I didn't want to co-sponsor this club. Snod Ass talked me into it."

"What if you called him Snod Ass and he walked around the corner?" Malone stopped and picked up some trash on the hallway floor, crumpled it up, then threw it in a nearby trashcan. Two janitors with their janitorial carts nodded in reverence.

"You just called him that."

"Are you going to see Elizabeth at practice today?" she asked.

"Malone, of course I'm going to see her today. Did you forget that you had me make her the manager of the team? Boy, was that a great idea! Have a Down's kid the manager of a varsity basketball team. Grand idea. Do you know I have to do everything now. She doesn't do anything I ask her to do—"

She stopped in her tracks. "Carrie Tomlinson. You are the dork here…not Elizabeth. I asked you specifically if you thought it would be a problem. Christ Almighty!"

"Christ Almighty is right. Malone—stop." I reached and grabbed her elbow and she shook me off. "Don't give me the slip, Malone. I'm already reeling over a broken heart."

"Yeah, but I'm not the one who broke it, Carrie. You need a haircut and start eating some more will you? You've lost too much weight."

I rolled my eyes. "This is great. We're having a spat. You and I are having a lover's quarrel and we haven't even gotten to the first date."

Under her breath, "Nor will we ever!"

"You sting me, Audra Malone. I'm not that bad."

"Your slut-o-meter is even higher than that Shane girl's on *The L-Word.* Jesus, you even look like her, except you don't dress like a hobo. You give men a good name."

"You're comparing me to her. Thanks, but no thanks," I

said.

"God, even before you were with Susan, I heard rumors that you were quite the Lothario, always going for only the hottest of the hot."

"A Lothario and a hobo," I laughed. "I'm so in love with you and we get to now go in and co-sponsor the GSA together. Queer teachers unite. Do you want to marry me?"

We turned the corner and ran smack into the principal: Evan Snodgrass. In a brown suit and wing tips, he sneered a gentle sneer and put his arm across his chest and his hand to his chin as if he were pondering an algorithm. "Ms. Malone. Ms. Tomlinson. How goes it with your new club?"

The smart-ass in me escalated. "Very well. Today we are tackling gay marriage, the Bible and how schools are unsafe for homos like Malone and me."

Laughing and looking to the floor, he shifted. "Okay, what are we really doing. This is the one club I am going to have to watch carefully this year."

Audra, the clack-dish, perked up. "Well, Mr. Snodgrass. We are just meeting for the second time. We have about five members and we're just getting the format down for what we want to do to help bridge gaps and break barriers."

He shuffled again. "Well, as long as we don't break too many barriers. The only reason this got off the ground is because my wife's brother is a gay preacher. He's had quite the influence on her. And, well, she's really tried to get things evened out since her parents disowned him. Crying shame they are dead and can't see what he has become. You all have a good year with them. Oh, and Ms. Malone, how's Melissa Fortunata doing in your class?"

"Fine—why?"

"Her mother called into the guidance office today worried that she may be spending too much time with one of your students…hmmmm."

I sounded in the Cichetti alarm. "Elizabeth Cichetti?"

"Yes. How did you know?"

"Just a hunch…I get them sometimes."

Mr. Snodgrass began to walk away down the west wing corridor. "Well, keep an eye on her and the other one. Evidently, there was a note passed to Melissa Fortunata that sounded like Elizabeth wanted to marry her or something like that. Weird. But, I guess you two can handle it."

When we got to Malone's classroom, our five students were sitting atop desks looking more bored than forever waiting on itself. As we opened the wooden door, Elizabeth jumped up from a blind spot near the chalkboard.

"Mith Tomlinthon!" she screamed and her arms were up in the air like a V. She really was cute. Even though I couldn't keep track of her, her adorability-o-meter was quite high.

I rolled my eyes at Malone. "Hey, Cichetti…what's your favorite food?"

She looked at Malone and then she said, "Thpaghetti!" she spat with her tongue.

"And what's your dad's name?" I was getting her riled up.

Malone put her book bag down and under her breath told me to stop it.

"What?" I asked.

"The iambic pentameter rhyme fest."

"Eddie!" Elizabeth screamed.

"That's right. Eddie Cichetti. You are a poet Elizabeth Cichetti."

Elliott Brisbane came sauntering up to the two of us. His T-shirt was up to his nipples and he had a belly button ring proudly displayed. His hair was half-mohawk, half-moby dick. He had a huge six-inch piece that twisted out like a long tuft and parted the third eye all the way down to his nose. He was a senior and the boisterous voice of the GSA.

"Where you all been? We're beginning to think you forgot us?" He reached up and did a twist on the tuft between his thumb and index finger.

Malone shifted some papers on her desk, "Hey, everyone. Sorry we're late. We had a chat with the principal for a few minutes and that was at least one of the reasons."

Claire the baby-dyke Austin, whose red hair was deeper than pomegranate, came up to Malone's desk. "That's cool, Ms. Malone. You had some important matters with Snot-grass, we're sure." For a second, I thought she might be flirting with her.

"Snodgrass, Claire, there's no t."

"Whatevah!" She flipped her hair and went back to the desk next to Vivian Johnson, the other baby dyke but with dark brown hair neatly cropped at the sides.

Thunder Bucknell sat with his arms folded on his desk. His biceps bulged and his jeans had a chain wrapped around them. He was the Adonis of the boys and was humble and quiet, the opposite of the nickname given to him the day he was born by his drunk father who wouldn't let anyone, including his wife, call his son anything else.

"Mith Tomlinthon?" Cichetti pulled on the tails of my white Nordstrom shirt. She then put her hand down my pocket looking for candy or something. "Can I go to the gym and shoot? Please?"

She knew this was a point of contention with me. She was always asking to shoot. It was her secret harbor; her secret haven. She pulled out one of my flippy frogs and played with the webbed feet. "Can I go outside and sit on the bench near the brook?" This really meant she would go to the gym, but, at times, I'd actually located her by the bench near the brook.

"We need to have our meeting first and then we can go to practice. Just give it a few minutes. Okay?" I muffed her head with my hand and glanced at Malone who was writing something in a folder at her podium. Her room's bulletin board had a world map stuck in the middle and the countries were marked in large letters. There were tables for arts and crafts and the smell of Elmer's glue was still hanging in the air. There were boxes of crayons and pens and Sharpies. Two sides of the room had different flags: one for Virginia, the other for the USA. Yielding to myself for a moment, I decided to size up Malone for the eight hundredth time. She was pretty in a sort of way and if I had been attracted to her, I would have asked her out long ago. But,

I wasn't, so I hadn't.

"P-a-h-lease?" Cichetti tried to muff my hair but was too short to reach the top of my head. Instead, she hugged my leg and gazed up at me. On inspection, I saw her cracked lips and handed her my Chapstick. Cichetti giggled, uncapped the lid, and swirled it on her lips like she was a movie star.

"Let her go, Ms. T. She really wants to see if Melissa Fortunata is in the gym. They've got this DS slash EMR connection at the hip like they're twins or something." Claire Austin picked at her ear and looked at Vivian who had given her a stare of suspended disbelief.

"DS slash EMR? When did you start learning acronyms, Claire?" I sat down at a desk near the front and swiped my Chapstick back from Cichetti. She leaned into me and held my hand and twirled one of the silver rings on my right hand.

Thunder shifted in his seat. "Can we talk about the November dance that's coming up? I want to know if we can bring a date and if it'll be cool with the punks and the neo-Nazis and the Squids and the Snakes and Latin Kings if we do so?"

"Down Syndrome and Educably Mentally Retarded is what she meant." Malone looked at Vivian and then at me and crossed her eyes. I laughed.

Vivian stood up and stretched and picked up a pair of scissors to cut into a sheet of paper. "Cichetti and Fortunata are doing the eye thing, Ms. T. and Ms. Malone."

"The eye thing?" Malone looked at Vivian, who was my best point guard on the basketball team.

"You know." And she bugged her eyes out at Malone and then at Cichetti.

Cichetti asked me again, "Can I shoot? Please. Fortunata is there and waiting for me."

"Then absolutely NOT!"

Thunder rolled his eyes at Elliott, who was twiddling his hair into Rastafarian land and slumped far down in his seat at the back of the classroom. "Let her go, Ms. T. They like each other in a cute and retarded kind of way."

"Thunder, if I ever hear you say that again, I will remove your biceps and sew them to your chest so you look like a twitty fag…" Vivian Johnson was pointing a finger at him.

"Okay, that's enough, you two." Malone handed out the folders. "We're trying to reduce hate, not enforce it. Okay, Viv? Thunder…the only thing that is retarded in that statement you made is the lips from which it issued. Don't screw up your next kiss by drooling all over him."

"I don't know, I kind of like what Viv said and…" I shut up when I saw Ms. Malone shoot me the look of death.

Cichetti was moping. I got up and went to the door and finally gave in. "Elizabeth Cichetti. Go directly to the gym and get two of the players, Janet and Cody, to help you get the basketballs out and you can shoot. If Fortunata is there, then you can shoot with her, too."

Before I could get the "If Fortunata" out, she was gone— running down the hallway toward the gym. She pulled her pants up as she ran out and laughed and stole my frog, too.

"Okay, let's get this meeting started." Malone was back at her podium and our after-school meeting began.

My girls would warm up with my assistant and I would get to practice late, but I had promised Malone I would be here. I didn't like it. I wasn't sure how the student body or the faculty and parents were going to take this new GSA, but they were forming at schools across Virginia and had been for years. The students, like Thunder Bucknell, and teachers like Malone, really wanted it…not just Snodgrass. Malone was the one that knew all about the laws and rules of how to be a dyke or a fag in the state of Virginia. I really could have cared less. I never felt like any of it had ever applied to me. Just go out and date whatever woman came along with my twelve-pack of beer, and I was set. Twelve-packs and girls and I was in. I glanced out the darkening window to Sterling Road and imagined getting out. My skin felt thick and I wanted a drink.

Malone started by saying, "I need a few volunteers to help me with Lobby Day coming up in February. I know it's far off, but I need some people to come with me. Any takers?"

Thunder Bucknell turned a bit in his seat and said, "I bet Elizabeth Cichetti would do it. Seems she gets her way most of the time. Can we talk about the dance?" He glanced at me and I rolled my eyes at him.

When I arrived at the gym thirty minutes later, half my team was lying around on the gym floor, my assistant was in the coach's office on the phone, and Cichetti was underneath the bleachers with Melissa Fortunata, holding hands, giggling and smooching.

This was the gayest I'd ever seen anything.

# Chapter 4

When I got home from our lame-ass practice, which resulted in me finding Cichetti and Fortunata at the bench outside by the soccer field playing flippy frog frenetics, I decided it was a Friday night in October and the ethereal voices on the winds of rhyme and reason were calling me to go out and blow off some steam. The narrow road from my house passed by Audra Malone's bungalow: a quick five-minute drive from my best friend with railroad tracks in between and a small one-lane bridge. It was good when I needed to chat or have a beer or have someone to help me with the dishes. Malone was always stopping in half unannounced and vacuuming and doing my dirty dishes. My best friend at school and at home. Reddi-wip. Not tonight.

So, I called three of my drinking buddies since Malone was an avowed AA'er and told them I needed to vent my newly found lesbian woes, Simpleton and the Simpletons, with them at Ray's

Café. It was Charlottesville's only rainbow club and it was usually a mixed variety of gay, straight, and now probably the newly lovingly retarded. I wasn't sure how to handle this new love affair between Cichetti and Fortunata but would call Malone over the weekend for a discussion on Down Syndrome and EMR. My own retardation was that I was a teacher and didn't have an ounce of training on any of it and thought she could give me some insight. When I saw them at the bench earlier, it was all I could do to pull them away from each other and get back to the gym. The Fortunatas, who had been anxiously waiting to pick up their daughter, were unhappy that I could not find either one of them. I told them it was just a little mishap of losing them both to a bench and a green frog and that it wouldn't happen again. Nate Fortunata, Melissa's father, slurped in some spit when he talked to me from his wheelchair outside of their beat-up Buick and I couldn't make out a thing he was saying. Like father like daughter. An oxygen tank lay underneath and his nose was tubed up so he could handle his intake of air.

Fortunata did say one thing semi-clearly to Cichetti before she left that night. It was something like "Bye. Good. Green." I wasn't sure since Malone had told me she only knew about ten words anyway. God. They were both trapped in their heads. I didn't see—couldn't see how either set of parents dealt with the formidable frustrations of living with a special needs person.

"You're a special needs person!" Sammie yelled at me. Sammie Jessup was my old diesel-dyke buddy from childhood. "Jesus, Carrie. I could have told you that. You've been on your own short bus for as long as I've known you. That girl over there is in graduate school at UVA."

The acrid smell of smoke filled my lungs as I scanned the crowd. The neon lights in the window had a lit-up rainbow swirl and the tiny bar had a row of wooden stools at the bar where baby dykes and lipstick lesbians hovered over their drinks in search of something either funny or philosophical to say. On the dance floor at the end of the bar, four girls were paired off dancing to a slow song by Melissa Etheridge. The booths that lined the side of the place had high backs and the tables were rounded off at the corners for easy entrance and exit. All the booths were filled and the place was full as well, almost two deep at the bar. Spotting the one Sammie was cajoling me toward, I took a swig of beer and let the bubbles fill my throat and the warmth of it slowly line my belly.

"She's cute," I said. "But, I'm swearing off women till the next ice age. I feel about that frigid anyway."

Sammie shrugged her athletic shoulders. The thick black corduroy shirt she wore was untucked and her cowboy boot hit the top of the table as she crossed her legs. Her face was wide and square and German. Her blue eyes were close together and her nose had a small hook at the end where I imagined she could probably hook it under a beer tab and open it.

Prissy Charlotte, my other friend from my running club I missed every other Saturday, came in and sat down. "Hey, you two skanks." Charlotte was tow-headed and screamed half-femme, half-butch depending on what clothes adorned her attitude for the occasion.

I bristled. "How did I suddenly become a skank, you whorish, slut-like Tower of Babel?"

"Tower of Babel?" Charlotte inquired. "More like Tower of Tits. Honey, how much tighter can you get that tank top of yours under that shirt?"

"Shut it. Both of you. I like this top. It makes me feel as femme as femme can be."

Sammie rolled her eyes and poured beer into her glass. "Well, Carrie and I are as butch as Butch Cassidy can be. How are those boots feeling, you sexy Frigidaire you?"

Swallowing hard, I got up to order another beer. "I'm two-stepping tonight," I announced and finished off my beer. I slammed it on the table. "And, I am daring the both of you to dance with me. I've had a hell of a week. My team can't put the ball in the hole and I've got two retarded girls in love with each other."

"For God's sake, Carrie—you can't call them retarded!"

Charlotte stood up and hit my shoulder.

A fast song came on. I glanced at the young girl again. Simpleton off the brain—now a young one on the make. The alcohol was increasing my desire and my sangfroid. Such a dumb word no one understood. Maybe I could use it on the chick: how cool was that?

"Ow! Why?" I said, grabbing my shoulder. "That's what they are and they were holding hands and kissing under the bleachers during practice today. I'm so mad that Malone made me make her my manager. I love the kids, you know, but I don't know how she talked me into it."

"Is Malone still single?" Sammie asked.

"Yes. Why don't you ask her out? She's been riding the single rail for years…"

Sammie elbowed Charlotte. "Why have you never asked her out?"

"Me and Malone? I'm not attracted to her. Go for it, Sammie. You need a date yourself." Charlotte scooted in and put her long blond hair in a clip. "You should ask her out. She's not a big looker, but at least she has a decent job and a house. That sure beats the trailer you live in and that dumb-ass job you have."

The bar's *boom, boom, boom* began to vibrate everything in my body, including my nipples. The smoke wafted to the ceiling and everyone was either face down in their beer or scanning the crowd for a potential something—be it a dance, a kiss, a lay, or just a drink and some company.

Sammie stood up and pressed her shirt down with her thick hands. "You're right. Driving that produce truck for Dickie Hicks is pretty lame. But, at least it pays the bills."

"Here's her number. Call her!" I jotted it on a matchbook and handed it to her.

For the next three hours I tried not to say the word "retarded" and kept thinking about Simpleton, although I tried to focus on anything but her including the cash register, the ancient bartender and the backs of my fingernails. My stomach dropped every time I thought of her and about the billionth time I did,

I got up and asked the cute graduate student from UVA to do a two-step. Luckily, she said yes, otherwise I would have walked out and driven home drunk with one hand over one eye. A habit I was used to doing. Her nose had a silver ornament hanging in her nostril and her skin so many piercings the rest of her face appeared as if it had been stapled by a nail gun.

"What's your name?" I asked the student, twirling her around in a circle and trying to keep the quick, quick, slow, slow up without stepping on her Chuck Taylor shoes.

"Tree. My friends call me Tree. It's really Nancy, but they call me Tree."

"As in Oak Tree?" I shifted her around a tight corner.

"I grew really fast when I was younger and everyone started calling me that. When I got to my height now, which really isn't that tall, as you can see, I stopped growing but the nickname stayed. What's yours?"

"Bush. My friends call me Bush. It's really Carrie but my friends called me that because my pubic hair came in really fast..."

"Wait," Tree said.

"What?" We stopped on the dance floor.

"Are you making fun of me?"

"No, what are you, retarded or something? I thought you went to UVA?"

She walked away. And my Bush joke never even got to the part where I talked about a trim. I'd pissed her off but I didn't care. Shrugging I crookedly walked back to my booth.

"I'm going home. Sammie, can you give me a ride in the produce truck?"

Sammie rolled her eyes at me and got up. "Y'all keep my seat warm and I'll be back in twenty minutes."

"Thanks, I'm done with this place." I threw down thirty dollars for the tab.

Charlotte put her hands in the air. "That's too much, Carrie. You always leave too much."

"I don't care, Charlotte. Why don't you go dance with staple gun over there? I just called her retarded—I'm so sangfroid!"

"Don't use big dumb words around me." Charlotte hit me in the shoulder again. Then I hit Sammie in the shoulder and then Sammie hit Charlotte in the shoulder. An Indian compact cemented by our own stupidity.

I bobbled a quick-quick out of the bar with Sammie by my side. "We have to drive by Malone's house," I said. "Want to stop in? She's probably eating popcorn and watching a romantic movie. You really should think about it."

"I will. You've been drinking a lot lately, Carrie. Is your ex-lady still up your craw?" Sammie held my bruised shoulder as she guided me through the pickup trucks, the Jeep Wranglers and the Subarus.

We climbed into the salad and fruit truck and I answered, "My craw hasn't been the same since she broke up with me. I thought for sure she was the one—"

"Usually the sexpots are never The One. I dated this girl from Middlesex County one time. Her name was Ursula. No shit. Ursula. Ursula from Middlesex. When she told me that, I thought for sure that she was the one. Oh my. I've never had such wild things happen in the sack..."

"Really, like what. Were there whips involved and gigantic vibrators she strapped to her holster? Did she ride bareback with nothing on but her boots and her cowboy hat?"

Sammie crinkled her nose. "Oooo. Now I'm feeling like I'm getting a yeast infection from that visual. Ow. No, it was none of that. She just knew how to use her mouth in ways I'd never experienced."

Sammie drove as I leaned my head against the cool glass of the window. The dark trees flipped by as the speed increased—everything was the same in the dark.

I said, "Simpleton was the same way. I'd never experienced it in that way before. Okay, we have to stop talking sex."

"Why, that's all you ever want to talk about."

"Fuck you!"

"Fuck you, too!"

"I love you. Thanks for the ride." We'd pulled into my small four-room bungalow on the side of Jackson's Ridge and I nearly fell out of the side of the produce truck.

Sammie said she was going to stop by Malone's on the way back to Ray's Café but I did not want to talk anymore. My talker was talked out and my feet hurt from the boots and my quick-quick, slow-slow dancing inabilities with the stapler girl.

Once I was inside, the phone rang. It was Sammie saying fuck you again. I said it back and then hung up laughing. I half wanted to talk to Malone but would call her in the morning. She'd become my best friend but I did not want to bother her... especially if the salad truck was going to show up at midnight.

I did the spaghetti dishes that seemed drunk themselves, crusty and red in the sink from the night before, and gazed through the dirty pane of the window with a drunken rawness and saw my muddled reflection in it. My dark, short wavy hair was long in the front and short in the back. With wet hands from the faucet, I put my hands through its thinness and wiped my face clean dragging my fingers over my red green eyes that were too close together. My lower jaw was square like a man's and I had thin lips that pooched out from my splotchy face. I smiled wide at myself and looked at the large ivories that set even and neat in my upper and lower jaw. Then, I poked out my tongue at myself and swirled some more soapy water through the travel mug I carried with me everywhere. Fuck you, I said in the window. Fuck you for being so stupid about a girl from stupid Charlottesville.

Then I thought of Susan. The love of my life. Now it all made clear sense in my drunken state. Her picture was on my windowsill along with an assortment of stones and shells and Scout's paw print. My dog had died two years ago. Her paw print was cast in white plaster that took the form of a heart. Her tags lay in the middle. Staring at Susan's picture on the windowsill, I knew just what to do in crises like this.

I called Malone.

"Do you know it's midnight? For Christ's sake, I'm half asleep," she said answering on the second ring. Her voice sounded raspy and sweet.

"Is there a book on your chest?"

"Yes. What's wrong Carrie?"

"Susan was the love of my life."

"Are you drunk again?" Malone asked.

"Yes."

"I'm hanging up, then…" she said, half-yelling into the phone.

"Why? You don't care? Nobody cares anymore. Not even me."

"Carrie, I care…but it's the same story two or three times a month. You call me. You talk about Susan and then you end up babbling about her brother and how cancer is killing the world and then for some reason, you talk about Susan as if you think you could have saved her from that accident. Oh my God…"

"What?"

"I'm standing in my front bathroom at the window. There's a big produce truck in my front yard. Oh, now it's pulling out. For a second it scared me."

"I'm hanging up…you don't care, Malone. You never have cared about me…"

"Now comes the pity party."

"I know. What's wrong with me?" I asked.

There was a pause. Then, "Carrie. Go to sleep. We'll talk in the morning. Okay? I'll buy you coffee at Stir Crazy and you can tell me all about Susan and whatever girl just walked away from you at Ray's."

"How did you know?" I pleaded.

"Because you always call me when some girl walks away from you looking for answers. The big answer tonight is GO TO SLEEP. I'll pick you up in the morning."

"Malone?"

"Yes?"

"You're always picking me up, aren't you?"

She hung up on me and I managed a laugh before I sank down to the kitchen floor and fell asleep.

§

Stir Crazy was the coffee bar we frequented most on Saturday mornings. It was like most coffee places of the twenty-first century. Espresso this, machiatto that, and all kinds of homemade breads, cookies and brownies. The clientele was made up of your average UVA crowd getting a cup of joe-to-go for the game before they tailgated all afternoon or it was your dual-income-no-kid family getting ready for a day of fun at the park or the Barracks Road shopping center. You could smell the coffee bar from the time you left your car till it smacked you in the face coming in. When Susan was alive we came here most Saturdays to start our day. I still came down but my buddies joined me instead.

Fifi Charlotte always looked fifi when she wasn't acting butchy. That's what I'd decided to call her, especially since she had a clip in the back of her hair. Malone sat down with two lattes but Charlotte drank from her water bottle. She'd just done five miles around Rivanna Park and was staying away from high calorie coffee.

"So. Feef. Are you training for a marathon or something?" I asked.

"No. Butch. I'm just trying to stay in shape. I put on ten extra pounds last year from eating chocolate, drinking lattes." She signaled to our cups. "And eating mint chocolate chip ice cream—"

"Mint chocolate chip," Malone interrupted, "that's my favorite."

"Give me two of these lattes a day and that's all the sugar I need," I said.

"That's all the caffeine you'll need, too." Charlotte retied her shoe. "So, Sammie said she did some extra produce stops last night."

Malone cocked her eye at me. "This isn't for Dickie's Produce is it? What's going on, Carrie? You didn't mention any need for a late night salad last night on the phone."

"I was hoping you might want a late night tossing of the salad, Malone," I said, then rolled my eyes at Charlotte. "Come on. We've talked about Sammie before to you. She was just doing an obligatory drive-by. We all do them. Even I do them."

Charlotte exhaled, "I don't. I stopped after that Carol girl took out a stalker's warrant on me. I don't know why she did that."

"Because, Fifi, you were hanging on her curb all night long and you walked her to her car every morning with your cell phone to your head trying to reach her that way, too."

Malone threw her head back and laughed a snarky laugh. "Charlotte, I must admit you were a little mad about that girl."

I drew in a long sip of coffee and rubbed my eyes. "Who hasn't been smitten lately. Even the special ed. kids at school are going at it. I can see the headlines now written by my fifth-period class: Two Retards Falling in Love. Two Lesbian Retards at Sterling Road High School in Charlottesville, Virginia. I mean, I know it's bad to say retard but that's exactly how they are going to handle it if we don't squelch the lovebirds in some way."

Charlotte drank more from her water bottle. "You've got a good point, Carrie. You guys are going to have to run with this one. Stop it while you can before it gets out of control. Remember when it got out of hand with those two old ladies with the still behind their house? Good grief! It was like something from a Walton's rerun. It took a year for that one to die down."

Malone put her hands through her thick hair and looked at Charlotte, who raised her eyebrows, and then looked at me. "What?" I said.

Malone exhaled deeply. "After you left the meeting yesterday, we talked about the November dance and Thunder and Elliot are worried about what the faculty and staff might think if they show up with dates. They also want to dance with each other and Vivian and Claire said the same thing. The policy on same-sex dancing is a no-no. It's a real concern for them and I want to talk about it at the faculty meeting next week. Can you back me up?"

Malone sipped her coffee while Charlotte inspected her pinky nail then bit into it and looked at me.

I put my arms in the air in a long, hungover stretch. "I don't know, Malone, it's hard enough for me to keep my presence around the basketball players and their insanely conservative parents while I'm on the GSA team. I'm not sure I can make it all year on this committee without some fallout myself."

Charlotte blew a remnant of her nail to the floor and then contemplated it for a minute. "It's 2009, for crying out loud, can't we get past this self-imposed hatred?"

"What do you mean self-imposed hatred?" I asked. Malone patted Charlotte on the back.

"Our own worst enemies, Carrie, are ourselves. You should know that by now. You're the pontificating English teacher who writes the poetry." Charlotte resumed the nail biting and raised her eyebrows at the both of us.

Malone looked surprised. "You write poetry? I didn't know you did that."

"Okay, I'm getting irritated with you two. No, I will not back you up. Yes, I write some poetry on the side."

This intrigued and pissed Malone off all at the same time. "Well, we have the dichotomy here, now don't we. An English teacher who has feelings for the written word but not for her students."

Charlotte blew out another nail remnant. "Sammie is really cute, Malone. You should give her a call. I've got her number."

Malone was still looking at me.

"What?" I said.

"Well then you don't need to be a co-sponsor of the GSA if I'm not going to get any backup at the faculty meeting next week."

"Fine. I quit. Can we go back to being nice to each other now?"

"She's got long hair and is a little rednecky, but I think she's worth checking out." Charlotte was not paying attention to either one of us.

Malone sipped from her latte. "Carrie, have you been to the Charlottesville Home?"

"No, but I have heard of it. Isn't it just right down the road near Ruckersville?"

"Yes. It's not far. I think we should go. I take River there every weekend to visit the residents."

"Why?" I asked. Two women I'd seen at the bar the night before walked in. I checked to see if staple girl was with them. The signs all over the walls were ones of African countries: Kenya, South Africa, Zimbabwe—coffee hat tricks for America.

Malone jabbed me in the left shoulder. "The Charlottesville Home houses adults with mental disabilities...from Down Syndrome to every type of retardation, to some adults who are multiply-handicapped and are in wheelchairs. I take River there to visit the patients. Some service dogs actually live there with the patients."

"River's such a good girl," I said. "But why do you want me to go and quit hitting me in the shoulder—both of you?" I eyed them both with suspicion.

Malone went on, taking a nibble from her scone, "Because I talked with Fortunata's parents and they are thinking about letting her live there after she graduates this June. Evidently Nate has got COPD and and the mother, Gwendolyn, is going to be the sole breadwinner. He can't work anymore and it's going to be too hard to keep Fortunata around. Plus, it's fun to watch River in action. She's a great therapy dog. I never knew German shepherds were so smart."

"Oh, that's tough." Charlotte was paying attention now and muttering. The crowd waxed and waned and we were trending toward being the only ones in Stir Crazy. Good Indian name, I noted.

"What does Gwendolyn do for a living?" Malone asked me.

I scooted closer to her. "She's a midwife and a part-time farmer. The Fortunatas live up route 158 in the trailer park behind the hill from Sterling Road High School. Malone, you should know that. Dork. Was Fortunata around while you all were talking about the Charlottesville Home?"

"Yes, she was. We had to walk up to the gym because she

was shooting most of the time with Elizabeth Cichetti. Melissa Fortunata's parents came in fifteen minutes beforehand to pick her up. That's when they must have gone behind the gym and out to the bench by the soccer field. Carrie, I can't believe you didn't see them do that."

I rolled my eyes. "Malone, I care more about the drills my point guard and wing girls are doing than keeping track of them. It's too much. God, my team went through the same basketball drill for forty-five minutes last night. Not one layup. Not one! One ball banged off the backboard so hard then hit me in the back of the head when I was showing Cody how to dribble with both right and left hands. I made them run ten suicides in a row for that plus a foul shooting percentage that was so low I couldn't even believe it." I slouched down in my chair and looked at the pictures of Africa again. Run away to Africa seemed to be an appropriate message.

Malone continued ignoring my basketball grief. "I tell you, they are the weirdest people. Nice, but weird. The father has his pants way too tight and the mother walks with her head down mostly like her neck hurts. They look like something out of a James Dickey novel. *Deliverance*. I'm not sure if he's brushed his teeth this year."

Charlotte swallowed more water from her bottle of water. "How do these kids get to stay after school? When I was in school, I had to get on the bus and get home to do my chores. No passing go, no collecting two hundred dollars."

Malone wiped coffee from her mouth and took another sip. "Elizabeth had somehow gotten her to stay unbeknownst to the Fortunatas who weren't too happy she was hanging around the little dyke. They do let her walk home but want her home before it gets dark. She takes the trail right behind the school. Right, Carrie?"

I repeated "the little dyke" and laughed and Charlotte shoved my shoulder. "Malone, I can't believe you said that." I looked around for the little retarded dyke police.

Then I shoved her back.

The place had suddenly filled and every table in the coffee shop was taken and the baristas were barking at each other. Every now and then it was a double frappacino latte here, a triple latte there, a no whip cinnamon dolce lovers espresso chocolatta. Coffee had become a whole new language and tea wasn't far behind: chai tea, mint-white puffy walnut tea, gizmottoa from African Root berry tea, Chinese Infusion Russian Scottish Earl Grey.

I didn't tell this to Malone, but the Fortunatas had been a bit irritated when they saw that Melissa and Elizabeth were hanging out shooting hoops and then by how I couldn't find them afterward. I was hot and sweaty myself from posting up with two of my senior forwards, Jenny and Colleen, at the opposite end of the gym when they arrived. Both were over six feet tall but neither possessed the knowledge that they were closer to the basket than most people. Egads. Part two of the basketball graveyard.

"You know one thing, Malone?" I asked.

"What?"

"I didn't realize until they showed up that Fortunata can't say much. What's wrong with her?"

"She's verbal but we're not sure why she only uses two-to three-word sentences when we know she can do more. She has about ten words total that she uses. One time, her middle school teacher said she did almost three entire sentences together when she was in the seventh grade. But, for some reason, she's reduced herself to 'yes, no, please, more.' Words like that." Malone hit me on the shoulder.

"What's that for?" I asked.

Charlotte interrupted. "I know what that's for: you losing the girls, not noticing that about Fortunata. That's her name, right?" Malone nodded. "And, for just generally being a schmuck when it comes to what flies out of your mouth and not caring."

They bumped fists.

"So, that's why Fortunata writes notes to Elizabeth and Elizabeth writes them back. She's much more of a scribe than she is a speaker," I noted.

I pulled a pen from my pack and grabbed a napkin and scribbled on it. Then showed it to Charlotte and Malone. *Kiss My Ass.*

Malone threw her head back in mock laughter. "Oh, you are such the poet."

"Does anyone want to go to the movies today?" Charlotte inquired. "I really want to go and see that new one with Susan Sarandon and Helen Hunt. I can't believe it but I heard they actually kiss each other in the movie. Come on. We have to have some takers on this?"

"I'm out. I'm going home to write napkin poetry. Maybe tomorrow."

Malone got up from the table. "Well, I'm out too. I'm going to Richmond today to spend some time with my family."

"Oh, that's so sweet of you Malone. Why don't you come by on your way home and we'll do a movie and pizza."

"Cool. What time?"

"Seven o'clock. You bring the pizza and I'll bring the DVD. Charlotte, you can come by, too. Skip your movie and bring Sammie..."

Malone interrupted. "No, I'm not dating that truck-driving girl."

I laughed. "Now who's being the provincial one? I've got the mouth but you've got some narrow-mindedness, my friend. You need to get over that and under someone quick."

She stuck her tongue out at me.

Weirdly, something visceral happened deep in between my legs. I looked to the African portraits for an answer and then back to Malone.

"Are you going to use that?" Charlotte inquired and giggled.

"Oh, ha, ha!" Malone got up and threw her trash away.

Charlotte followed and dropped some napkins on the floor without notice. For a second, I thought I might reach down and pick them up but ignored them instead.

Saturday coffee with Charlotte and Audra Malone: the

precursor to my day of drinking. We loved our irreverence and counted on the banter every weekend. Malone was an exceptional special ed. teacher, known in Albemarle County to be one of the best. Me, I was just an average English teacher who could prevent the rednecks from killing the Goths—half the reason Malone wanted me on the GSA. She knew I could handle student friction well. The last fight on campus was between two black girls on the ramp in building eight. They called me down and I arrived just as some of the last hair extensions were being thrown into the hallway.

This year was a little different with my terrible fifth-period class. I could see it was going to be a struggle every day till the final bell sounded in the hot air of June to release them from my prison, not theirs.

# Chapter 5

On Monday morning, Elizabeth Cichetti came bounding and burbling toward me, half-hunched over and deliberate in hitting the concrete sidewalk in front of the main office. *Blam. Blam. Blam.* Her dark hair swung loosely as if it might tumble right off and her hands were balled into fists of Cichetti fury. Students parted like the Red Sea when they saw her face pinched like a prune and the spittle coming from her mouth. Evidently, the spittle was my name.

"Mith Tomlinthon. Mith Tomlinthon..." She stopped before me as I tried to sip from my coffee cup and she managed a Cichetti sigh. What now? What could be torturing the girl who always gave me the slip?

"What's wrong Cichetti? You're acting like the second coming is a-coming and you've got something to do with it. You need to hustle up and make your lunch announcement. It's almost eight twenty—" I looked at my watch, "and you know how Ms. Schindler gets when you are late. They're having your favorite dessert: fudgies."

"Fortunata. Fortunata. Fortunata." She stopped, out of breath, and put her hand in my pocket and pulled out the green frog I carried sometimes. "Fortunata is stuck in the bathroom and can't get out. She's stuck. The knob doesn't work. The boys. The boys. The boys." Her tongue jutted out and she was disheveled. Her white shirt was untucked in the back.

She couldn't get the rest of it out but I spilled my coffee as I threw it on the uneven sidewalk. "What are you talking about 'Fortunata is stuck in the bathroom?'" I grabbed her by her button-down shirt. She pulled her pants up and looked at the frog.

"Cichetti! Look at me!" I snapped.

"The boys," she said and looked down the walkway.

"Come on, Cichetti. Show me," I said and grabbed her hand and picked up a trot down the walkway by some students sitting in front of building ten. We were two large buildings away from the fountain and the boys' bathroom near building eight.

I'm not sure if it was Mr. Jack Doff or Tulio Grayson or one of their redneck neo-Nazi, hip-hop Latin Kings friends who decided to lock Fortunata in the bathroom. Cichetti told me that they were holding hands by the school's dried up fountain when these boys just started talking to them. I had visions of how they might be doing the talking: mocking a couple of exceptional ed students. Just the kind of gang initiation someone might need. Then I thought of what they might do to the both of them or now just to Fortunata.

"One told me he thought we were cute," Cichetti told me. "Then he asked if we wanted to thee something neat and then took us to the boy's bathroom near building eight. That's right near your room, Mith Tomlinthon." She was in and out of her lisp and she was breathing hard.

I myself had been holding Elizabeth's hand but dropped it and hustled ahead of her. Locked in a bathroom. God. What had

43

they seen? Who did this to two retarded girls? God, I've got to stop saying that word.

Cichetti lumbered to me from behind and grabbed my hand.

I reached back and returned the grip. She had her green frog in it. I could feel its plastic webbed feet dig into my hand. My mind continued to race with all kinds of weird thoughts. Ask Cichetti. I don't want to know. Oh, God. I need a Bloody Mary and first period hasn't even begun. Bloody Mary. First period. Fortunata. Holding hands. The Latino boys that hung around the gym. Finally, a voice inside said ask, ask, ask. You numbskull.

"What did they show you, Elizabeth?" I asked.

"I don't know. I don't know, Mith Tomlinthon. Is Fort okay?" She squeezed the webbed feet into me harder. "I ran to get you because they thaid it was something about locking us up and they all thtarted laughing and I laughed but then one of them grabbed Fort's hair and I ran to get you." Cichetti looked up at me like I was some kind of savior. Jesus H. Christ.

None of this was logical. Why would they be picking on Cichetti and Fortunata? Oh God. It hit me. The lesbian aspect. That was it. It was them holding hands and maybe they had tilted their heads against one another? Or maybe they just stood a little too close. The nuance too real that it had to be expunged by a rite of passage to a gang initiation. I ran ahead a little in my brown lacy Skechers and turned the corner to see a growing group of students in front of the boys' bathroom.

Elliott Brisbane saw me and darted over with his mohawk down and parted in the middle. Cichetti had her hand through my belt loop.

"It's locked, Ms. Tomlinson. Those fuckers locked her in there. We just heard her call out." Elliot stared at me then joined me in pursuit.

*Those fuckers* was right I agreed internally and let his four-letter word waft away in the air like I'd never heard it.

I rushed to the door all the while Cichetti staying hooked to me. "Cichetti, tell her to undo the pin. Elliot, go get an administrator and tell them to hurry. Claire…Claire?"

"I'm right here." She scooted in close to me.

"Go get Ms. Malone. Run. Run as fast as you can."

She looked funny. "Running is not allowed on campus."

"Run!" I yelled.

Claire took off and two of my basketball players, Juanita Jones and Robin Altoona, came up to see if they could help by getting on one another's shoulders and trying to peer through the open split window at the top of the door frame. Robin climbed atop Juanita's shoulders.

"You see her, Robin?"

"Naw, Coach T., I can't see nothing." Robin swayed around trying to catch a hopeful glance of something. Oh, the grammar of it all. Now we had mashed syntax.

Bloody Mary, I almost cussed but pressed it inside myself. What would Susan do? So, I yelled. Finally. "Melissa Fortunata! Hey, honey. We're here to help. Can you hear me?"

Then nothing. Nothing came from the bathroom. I jiggled the door then banged on the door.

The smell of stale urine permeated the air and the brick wall was inked with I heart someone and neo-Nazis rule and this school sucks. Sterling Road High School had blue balls because of a nameless girl from 1984. The echo of urinal flushers resounded in the air of the past where hundreds of local boys had come to take a piss and secretly eye the length of their bathroom buddies' cocks.

We all inhaled while Robin bobbled around on Juanita's neck. Cichetti pressed her head against the door and gently asked for Fort. She asked two or three times. *Fort. Fort. F-o-o-o-r-t.* Nothing. I heard nothing then jiggled the doorknob once more and leaned into the door. In the next few minutes while we waited for an administrator to come with a key, the silence got as loud as a screeching siren, a muffled scream, a hollow tunnel an ocean wave might crash into. An echo from the drip of the faucet could be heard and the wind waving through the trees that made distant shadows on concrete come alive in the nature of it. A

45

retarded girl locked in a boys' bathroom. What the perpetrators had done, no one knew but Fortunata.

At the edge of the cinder block wall, I peered up as I continued to hold Cichetti's hand. I had become the moron. Her other hand was pulling my shirt, gripping hard. There was a dark, creepy spider slowly scuttling toward a moth that was caught in its web. The moth was alive and vibrating its wings back and forth with all its might to get away from the sticky den of death it was annealed to. It shook violently as the spider drew near and then crawled on top of it. I saw napkins on a floor, pictures of Africa, a face peppered with metal balls, then warm beer in my belly.

Quickly, I glanced away and at Cichetti. I could not bear to watch the death of this moth as Melissa Fortunata lay on the floor in the bathroom. I prayed her clothes were still on. Looking up again, I saw the whole web shake violently as the spider tried to stick its venom into the moth. Then, the spider crawled away and I was positive the moth was dead. Bloody fucking Mary.

"What's going on here?" Mr. Snodgrass came up, fumbling with keys and then trying to get the right one out. His gut was hanging over his pants and his Blue Ridge Mountain Dog tie was askew. He had a buzzed head and his nose was splotched from too many Jim Beams at the close of his day.

Elizabeth dropped her frog on the ground and Claire came bounding back from getting Malone. I picked up the frog, handed it to Cichetti and momentarily forgot the moth's demise.

"Looks like some boys were trying to have some fun with Elizabeth and Melissa here and have gotten the biggest jolly by locking Melissa Fortunata in the bathroom," I ventured.

Cichetti dropped my hand and knocked on the door as Mr. Snodgrass inserted the key. "It's okay Fort, Mr. Thnodgrath is here to help. I've got something for you…"

Malone knocked on the door. "Melissa! Melissa honey? We're here. Remember—" Then Snodgrass jiggled the key. "What's wrong? Does the key not work?" Malone started to become a bit frantic. "Melissa does not like to have her routine changed. Being in there will make her clam up for three weeks or more. Can you hurry? She won't talk for three weeks, or worse…"

"Calm down, Malone," I said. "We're going to get her out."

Cichetti kept saying Fort over and over again.

"Carrie, you don't understand. It's taken her years to get the words out that she says now. She hates to be locked in. It's what happened when she was younger. She used to be locked in the bathroom when she wouldn't speak up. It was before they knew she couldn't speak at all."

Snodgrass got on his walkie-talkie. "Can we get a custodian to building eight's boys' bathroom?" A ten-four came back from the front office.

The eight thirty bell rang and the horde of students who had gathered around the bathroom didn't move. Some students were saying that they couldn't believe someone would lock a special ed. student in the bathroom. One of the preppy intellectual kids said they were a bunch of queer sickos. On that I yelled for the band of students to head to first period. Some drifted away slowly, others stayed to see what the outcome would be.

"Robin, get off Juanita's shoulders…she's going to have to be able to shoot." I said this and Robin got down. "Go on to first period. Thanks…I'll see you later."

Robin jumped down and came up to Cichetti. "Elizabeth Cichetti don't ya worry your purty little face. Fort's coming out. Just going to take awhile. Okay?"

Cichetti smiled at Robin and Juanita, shy and reserved yet clinging to me the whole time.

"Carrie—" Malone turned to me. "This is reprehensible. Who did this?" Then she looked at Cichetti. "Cichetti, who did this? Why would someone want to lock Fortunata up?"

Elizabeth Cichetti just shrugged and that's when I peeked back up at the spider which was back on top of the moth. It was almost like it was raping it and then I made a terrible correlation to Fortunata. Was this symbolic of what had just happened or had I read one too many of James Joyce's books? I got a vile sickness in my stomach. Simply, I could have simply reached up and stopped the moth from getting ravaged by the spider but did

47

not. Let nature take its course I thought. There was nothing I could do about it.

"The custodian is on his way, Melissa," Malone shouted through the door. "It'll be okay. We can do some finger painting of the horses after we get you out. Would you like that Melissa?"

"Look at the spider, Malone," I said sheepishly not wanting Cichetti to hear.

"What? What…" she asked, distractedly, patting on the door and saying it was all okay for the tenth time.

"Oh, for Christ's sake!" And then, she reached up and flicked the spider off the moth and then delicately with her index finger and thumb removed the prey from a sure death. The moth flew to the cinder block and clung to it.

"Aren't you afraid of spiders?" I asked, banging on the door again. The custodian came from around the corner with a crowbar and a hammer.

Elizabeth saw the weapons of mass destruction and looked at me and started hitting her head and squealing against the old testament of the graffiti wall. I grabbed her hands but she flung against me and started again. The sweat poured from my brow.

"Not to Fortunata! Not to Fortunata! Not to Fortunata!" she screamed and hit her head against the door.

"Dance with her," Malone said and then moved closer to us. I was dumbfounded, again, like the spider and moth had just put a spell on me. I was staring and befuddled all at the same time.

Malone cocked her head and looked at me funny. "Carrie— just rock with her back and forth. Can you do that?"

"Yes."

So, as Cichetti continued her hysterical hitting, I tried grabbing her arms again and again as Malone helped push the door in with Snodgrass and the custodian. I rocked like I was in a rocking chair and Cichetti resorted to twirling her hands around in conical circles. A habit some Down's people had. The rocking helped.

Finally, after fifteen minutes, the doorjamb released and the door flung wide open.

There was Melissa Fortunata sitting on the floor, her head down, looking at a piece of paper. The stench of urine lay thick in the air and the green and white tiled floor was chipped in a million places. The three urinals were opposite the two stalls. The dark green paint was etched in its own graffiti where students said more in a bathroom than in English class.

Then Malone worked her magic while Snodgrass and I tried to disband the group of students now late to first period.

Slowly, Malone walked up to her and then Cichetti pulled at me to go in, too.

"Hey, Melissa." Malone sidled up next to her. "Looks like we've had a rough morning. Getting locked in the boys' bathroom isn't something that's very fun. Why don't we get you out of here and we'll get your face cleaned up and have a snack. What do you think about that?"

Fortunata had a wide, Slavic face and her hair was mussed up and frizzy and down to her shoulders. The back of her hair was wet from what I thought at first was sweat, but on further inspection realized was urine. Her lips were wide and bulbous and her green eyes swollen and red from the crying. No words would come from her lips.

Then Malone asked the question everyone was thinking.

"Did those boys touch you honey? Did they put their hands on you in a way you wouldn't like?"

Malone looked at me as she put her hand to the back of her head and shirt. Urine. Malone smelled her hand and then put it back to the back of Melissa's head.

Slowly, Fortunata shook her head. Cichetti bent down and handed my flippy frog over to Melissa. She smiled a large, toothy grin and took it. She fingered its head softly and shyly looked up at Cichetti.

"It's yours Fort. My special frog. Okay?" She smiled and patted Fortunata on the head.

"Okay."

Fortunata said this and only this. And, this was good enough for all of us.

§

Later that evening, after what looked like a Keystone Kop basketball practice, I went for a jog with Charlotte at the trailhead to Campbell Park and told her the events of the morning. I could barely keep up with Charlotte as she ran like a deer on the trail. The trail lights illuminated our run and it felt good to breathe in the dark blue air. However, fifteen minutes into our run I told her to stop.

"Why we haven't even gone a mile and a half, Carrie. You need to rest here and I'll do a loop and come back." Charlotte zipped up her striped North Face jacket.

"No, I can keep up. I'm just so upset about what happened this morning. I'm convinced it was some of my criminals from fifth-period class. I need to sit down and talk about it for a minute. Reflect, you know?" Beside a large rock and the sign that said Campbell Park, I sat down on a bench looking for an answer in the air. Two slender gentlemen walked by and said hi. I waved at them.

Charlotte stretched and stroked her calves like they were iconic statues. "My legs are looking better, don't you think? And, you never reflect about anything, Carrie. The last reflection you did was into your margarita the last time I saw you. Get over it. Kids do crappy things to other kids. It happens all the time, every year in America. It's just a part of growing up. It's ingrained in our social history. We've all been through it. There's nothing to ponder. Let's go. Come on." She jumped up and then stretched her hamstrings, which she rubbed as she bobbed up and down like she was a pogo stick.

"Charlotte are you not listening. Your legs look great," I said, then got up from the bench. "Well, I'm just going to let Malone handle it. She's got both of them in class and maybe she can just get to the bottom of it."

"Push it off on her. Good idea. That's the way to reflect!" She tried to high-five me but I turned away to look at a pine tree instead. The branches coiled then recoiled in the wind that was stirring up a late October storm. Dark clouds swirled around us and a few squirrels scampered over the trail into the space where some brambles jutted out.

"Storm's coming," I said.

"Get your ass up then. I need to get this run in to start my week. Then I have to go to Sammie's trailer and fix her dinner for the week. I swear that girl needs a good woman. I wish Malone had at least a little interest."

"Malone doesn't know she's alive in between her legs. She doesn't feel."

Charlotte took a step closer to me. "You are kidding. Has she ever done it?"

"I think so."

"Well, you are her best friend. Why don't you ask her?"

"It's a tight subject. I think she just likes being asexual. There are those people, you know."

"Oh my God! I could never be one of those people. Do you think they are here—here in this place?" She looked around with her deer-in-headlights look.

"Charlotte, you are stupid. They're everywhere. Don't worry. They won't rub off on your legs or in between them."

"Funny. Really funny, Carrie," she said and sat down on the bench next to me.

"Speaking of being alive," I said and turned to Charlotte. "You ever thought about being dead?"

"Carrie, what's the gig, babe? You thinking about Susan too much?" Carrie wiped her brow then wiped mine trying to be sweet. I looked away again.

"I don't care about Susan anymore, Charlotte. You know that!"

"Of course you care about her. We all miss her, Carrie… especially Malone. We've all been best buds since college. You and Susan were inseparable." Charlotte crossed her legs and checked her fingernails.

I leaned back. "How about we go to Green Top Sporting Goods, get us a couple of revolvers and end it all."

"Okay. You want to go now. Do I have to kill you or do we

just commit suicide like normal people?"

"You don't have to kill me. I'll just do it in my house on the couch. It will be the couch-assisted suicide."

"Okay, since we are going to have a couch-assisted suicide, can I bring popcorn and a movie?"

"Yes. I'd like my last movie to be *The Sound of Music*," I said and then put my elbows on my knees.

Charlotte pondered. "I'd like my last movie to be *Priscilla, Queen of the Desert*. Talk about going out in a blaze of ABBA glory!"

"Sounds good to me. I'll get the popcorn."

"I'll get the movies."

"What day do you want to do the CAS?" I asked.

"CAS?" Charlotte looked at me.

"Couch-Assisted Suicide," we said in unison, then laughed like hyenas in heat.

Charlotte said, "I can tell Sammie to pick up the guns. She drives by that place all the time and we can do it as soon as we're feeling as shitty as shitty can be."

"Okay. Deal?"

"Deal!" Charlotte smacked me on the leg. "Now, let's get this run going. If I'm going to kill myself, I want to look decent in a casket."

"Well, if you blow your brains out, my dear, no one is going to be looking at your legs."

"Carrie, you are so stupid. For one thing, you don't give a shit about anything anymore. Secondly, you can't figure anything on your own anymore, except which college student you can fuck. And, third, you probably can't even write a suicide note even though you are an English teacher. Ever heard of that? Dork, I can kill myself with a revolver, but it can be a blow to the heart...body intact...open casket, full on for the legs."

"Charlotte, I can't wait to get on the couch with you!"

"Oh, God! Quit making suicide sound sexual. You dork."

"Everything is sexual to me—even death."

"You're so macabre!"

"Well, look at you with your vocabulary Ms. Charlotte. I die first." I ran ahead of her.

"No fair! I die first!" She came fast on my tail and passed me.

Charlotte was a good friend to want to die with me. Good friends were hard to come by these days.

# Chapter 6

After the bathroom prison break, I could only hope that things on Tuesday would get better and life would return to normal at Sterling Road High School. Hurriedly, I poured my coffee and ever so briefly looked at the picture of Susan precariously placed on the left corner of my kitchen window: my girlfriend of sixteen years. Dead.

I paused and rubbed my thumb over her tanned cheek. Where are you? Where are you now, Susan? Her curly brown hair delicate in the wind on the afternoon I took the picture outside by her favorite ancient swing.

Out the window, I looked at the yellow maple tree and the two ropes that wrapped around a strong branch that cupped a piece of flat board for a seat, our makeshift swing. There, many times, she had sat on my lap as we twirled around and around—her thighs heavy on mine and her heels kicking my shins. I made no bother ever to tell her to stop. Indeed, it felt ancient—so long since I'd seen her alive and thriving with laughter. For a moment, I could feel her behind me—wrapping her strong forearms around my waist and swaying to nothing, just the pulse of her own body, her own rhythm. Her cheek against my cheek and her perfume rising to my nose.

I closed my eyes and leaned forward. When I opened them, I reached out once more for the picture and whispered goodbye. Goodbye, goodbye, goodbye. Soft. Gentle.

I needed a drink.

Then, suddenly and without much reverence, I thought of guns and Green Top and Charlotte's and my couch-assisted suicide. We would have to decide on our last meals: perhaps steak, mashed potatoes and apple pie. This, suddenly, felt like prison both at school and underneath my skin.

On the way to school, I passed by Malone's house. Gone already. The leaves down Route 6 were turning true to the vibrancy of the Blue Ridge Mountains. I thought of Henry David Thoreau and Ralph Waldo Emerson and their relative testimonials on nature. Go to the woods. Live deliberately. Simplicity. Trust thyself. I could hear it on the spiritual voices of the leaves that turned from green to gold, then noted the irony of that very phrase: green to gold. My Jeep clunked along the road and I spilled coffee on my console. My thoughts regarded Fortunata and young boys pissing in her hair. I began to replay it over and over in my head. The leaves and the grass and the dirt outside gave me no answer to this.

But, what could I do? I was just an average teacher who wanted to think poetry and drink my life away. Why not? The rest of the writers did. Christ, look at Jack Kerouac—my twentieth-century idol. He drank himself to death and I understood why. Too much pain. And then I got mad at Susan for dying, leaving me with my dumbass teaching job, my dumbass sexual escapades, and my dumbass life. Then without warning, I cried.

Fuck.

When I arrived at seven forty-five, I found two of my

basketball players outside of my room. Each was leaning up against the door with crossed arms: not a good sign.

I fumbled with my keys and my leather portfolio that acted as a prop on weeknights and weekends. "Good morning. Are you guys ready to take on Albemarle High School tonight in our first game of the season?"

Terri Bouisseau, my point guard, and affectionately known as "Pickle," nodded then looked at the floor. Then, as I put the key in my door to open my classroom while clenching the Styrofoam coffee cup in my mouth, Vicki began babbling in her tenth-grade manner.

"Shut up, skank," Vicki said, elbowing Terri in the side.

"I didn't say nothing," Terri said back.

Terri frowned at her and then laughed nervously. "Ms. Tomlinson," Vicki continued, "we're a little afraid of something and need to talk to you about it."

"Oh, yeah," I said. "What's up? Come on in."

My room was small and could barely fit the twenty-eight desks that faced each other. I had a small podium up front with a wooden stool. In the back, my tired old desk from 1892 balanced itself on three good legs. The fourth leg was two inches off the floor and had a stack of Post-it notes holding it up.

The bulletin board had a poem by William Butler Yeats on it: "The Lake Isle of Innisfree." All over the board were plastic stars that illuminated when the lights were out. Three filing cabinets were stationed at the rear of the room near the window which faced Sterling Road. The window had blinds that were almost always raised so students could look out onto the courtyard that held the dried up fountain—the road was just past that.

The floor was the same as all the floors in the school, an institutional speckled concrete that was cracked at each corner in my room. The whiteboard had my writing on it. Neat and clipped like a good English teacher's should be. My objectives were all about writing epitaphs and preparing for poetry recitations. On my desk were some UVA wristbands that Cichetti had given me and there were some Tarot cards I played with when there was extra time in class. A whistle hung loosely on the back of my chair, along with a sports jacket, and a deflated basketball leaned against the side of my desk.

"Terri and I and some of the team members on the team are a little upset about the GSA that's forming and also what happened yesterday to Elizabeth Cichetti and Melissa Fortunata. Really, though, it's our parents who are up in arms. Some of the players told their parents that you were helping sponsor the GSA and that you were okay with what Cichetti and Fortunata were doing."

"Oh, Christ! I expected to hear some of this from my fifth-period crackheads, not my team members." I dropped my portfolio and peered over the top of my desk, then put my hand through my hair. "I'm just helping a little with Cichetti and Fortunata. You guys did just tell me that you know what happened yesterday to Melissa Fortunata. We talked about it at practice, right?"

"That's the other thing." Vicki seemed to be the leader on this. "We think it's kind of gross that they hold hands everywhere... and they are fawning all over each other...under the bleachers, in the locker room, and they went out yesterday and were hanging all over each other at the bench by the soccer field."

"Yeah," Terri interjected. "PDA isn't allowed in school. It's in the Code of Conduct."

"And," I said, "is calling someone a 'skank' not considered offensive in the Code of Conduct?"

"That's different. She said 'skank' in chest."

"You mean jest," I corrected. I put my coffee down and picked up my daily planner. Epitaphs. Great. More drudgery.

"Whatever." Terri sat at my desk beside me and began going through some of my papers.

"Terri, get your slimy hands off my papers. Skank. Ho. Poser. Freak. Snot-head," I said to her.

"No, you dih-int?" she laughed.

"If you're going to sit here, why don't you grade these papers. I don't feel like doing it." I said this and leaned back in my chair and looked out the window at Sterling Road. "Well, come on with it. What's the rest?" I asked. There was always more.

Vicki sat down next to Terri. "My dad commutes to Richmond every day and works for the two senators who put the Marriage Amendment in place for Virginia. If he sees them doing that stuff at a game or something or hears about you being on the GSA, he'll pull me and half the other girls off the team because everyone voted 'yes' to the amendment. Pickle and I are just trying to warn you."

I stared out the window a moment longer. Then a voice inside my head said give up, give up, give up. Snodgrass walked by my door and peeked in and waved, then walked out. Inhaling the last bit of java from the Styrofoam cup, I made my confession to my players.

"Well, I'm quitting the GSA. Don't you worry about that. I understand where you are coming from and I don't want to lose my team over that and Cichetti and Fortunata holding hands. Fort can't make it to the games anyway. Her parents won't let her. So, you all don't have to worry about that. Plus, Cichetti just wants to shoot the ball. She's not going to do anything that's going to distract anyone but me. Okay. So, don't worry. It's all under the carpet where it should be. You all just focus on your game, and leave the rest to me."

"Thanks, Ms. T," they said in unison.

"Oh, Ms. T.," Vicki said to me as she walked out the door. "We're glad that the straight teacher is off the alliance. For a minute, you had us worried."

For Christ's sake, my team thought I was the "S" in the Gay-Straight Alliance. How could that be? Were they really that naïve? Perhaps so.

Looking out the window, I burst out laughing. My team thinks I'm straight. Now, that was an abomination.

Poor Malone: exceptional ed and a dyke to boot. I'm sure they didn't mistake her. It was 2009, for criminal's sake.

Four minutes later, the real crime was committed.

No one saw it coming. Not Malone, not me, not the entire

faculty.

Four minutes later, Elizabeth Cichetti got on the loudspeaker to announce the lunch menu for the day. I surfed through my fifth period epitaphs to see what they would say about themselves if they could make their own gravestones. Sherry Proffitt's said:

Sherry Proffitt
1995 – 2009
Born free
Died Young
No Profit
Just Goth

Just Goth? What in the world was this...

A beep came over the loudspeaker. 8:20 a.m. I glanced at William Butler Yeats poem on the bulletin board.

I went to the next epitaph. Proffitt got a C for effort.

"Hello Thterling Road High Thchool. Home of the Blue Ridge Mountain Dogs. Thith is Elizabeth Cichetti and today for lunch...(I could see the attendance secretary pointing to the menu, placing each finger by the bulleted item). Today, it's pizza. That's Fort's favorite."

Behind Cichetti's voice, I could hear Peggy Schindler gently nudge her, "Go on, Elizabeth, read the next item."

"Pizza is Fort's favorite," she said again to Peggy. I could see the spittle on Cichetti's mouth. Looking through my window, I listened for the rest. The energy behind her words felt different.

Peggy said, "Well, I'm glad about that but let's go ahead and read the rest."

Elizabeth gurgled and snorted. I could almost see her rubbing her nose and fingering her orange UVA band. "French frieth. Chicken nuggetth. I like chicken nuggetth."

Peggy Schindler pressed her. "That's good. Now finish up with the rest."

And then it came.

"I love Fortunata. Even more than chicken nuggetth and thpaghetti!!! Fort, Fort, Fort! It's pizza Fort." She must have thrust her arms in the air while grabbing the mic at the same time.

I got up and walked to the window. Malone's room was about two hundred feet from where I stood. Come on, Malone. Come on, Malone. Show yourself to me. Hurry.

Suddenly, I saw Malone open her door. Good.

There was a screech on the microphone as Peggy struggled with Elizabeth to get it away from her. I heard another snort and then Elizabeth said, "I'm not done, Mrs. Schindler. I'm not done! I'm not done! I…"

"Yes, Elizabeth dear. I think you've said enough." Another screech and then I heard Snodgrass in the background say, "Hand me the microphone."

"NO!" Elizabeth barked. A chill went up my spine.

"Fortunata. I LOVE you!" She practically sang it into the loudspeaker. "Fortunata will you MARRY me? Will you MARRY me? We can have chicken nuggetth and french frieth and thpaghetti at the party. Will you Fortunata? Will you marry me Fort? Fort. Fort. Fort."

The whole school inhaled.

Every schoolroom on campus heard the pledge of allegiance of love that Cichetti had just declared. First it's the bathroom incident, and now we're going to the chapel. Who's going to lock her in there? God knows I was tiring of this. Charlotte's Couch-Assisted Suicide better come soon or I'd be getting in trouble next and I never got in trouble except with women.

Situational irony, here I come. I kicked my portfolio across the room and papers flew out of it. I had to run. And, run I did.

After the last blurp that came out of Elizabeth's mouth, I got to the office to get her to stop being so insanely obstinate about her gay agenda. When I got there, the microphone was turned off but Elizabeth thought Fortunata could still hear her, so she was talking away.

"We waited for Ms. Malone to come up here but she's got a class," Snodgrass said and rolled his eyes at me.

Cichetti was still blabbering away. "We can have balloons and play with your frog, Flip, and eat cake and ithe cream, Fort."

Elizabeth looked up and smiled at me with her toothy grin. She choked in her tongue.

"I've got her, Mr. Snodgrass. I'm on planning. Tell Malone that it's all right. I'll take her to class after I talk to her."

Peggy Schindler's hair was mussed up and she mouthed a thank you to me as I escorted Cichetti out the front door to the office and onto the sidewalk. A wind whipped up and I got a different chill this time. Out of the corner of my eye, I saw Sammie's produce truck on Sterling Road. She honked and we both waved. Making her run to Richmond I assumed.

"Mith Tomlinthon." She twiddled her arms and rolled her index finger and thumb together. Suddenly, I felt a twinge of empathy toward her. "Will you hold my hand?"

I grabbed Elizabeth's hand and we walked toward the gym and I hoped the auxillary gym was not in use and we could shoot for a few minutes and chat about her gay behavior.

Once there, I grabbed a ball and handed it over. It was like candy and she shot the ball underneath her legs and missed four or five times before she just began to bounce it with her tongue out. She bounced it in circles around the gym and she came up to me once and showed me her orange UVA band.

"Is that band for luck, Cichetti girl?" I asked. Two PE teachers opened the gym doors and saw it was just us and closed them up after I gave them a thumbs-up.

"Yeth. Where's yours?"

"Guess I need to get one. I think I have one on my desk."

"Luck is good," she said. "Lucky, lucky, lucky."

I muffed her hair. "Elizabeth." I tried to stop her from moving away from me, always how I lost her. She had no attention span and neither did I these days. She ignored me and continued to dribble with exuberant enthusiasm. "Elizabeth, I need to tell you some things and I hope you'll understand."

"Here, shoot with me, Mith Tomlinthon." She passed me the ball. I grabbed it and shot and missed. Damn. I hated to miss. The gym smelled like old sweat, and the district and regional banners on the wall for softball and baseball hung down in a dismal display of nostalgic sadness.

I stopped with the ball on my hip. "Okay, so, here's the deal, Cichetti. You can't be doing all of this that you are doing with Fortunata. It isn't right. You're holding hands and some of my players say you've been kissing her in the gym sometimes and now you've gone and asked her to marry her over the loudspeaker."

"Can we go see her? Mith Tomlinthon. I want to see Forty."

I kneeled down. "It's wrong, Elizabeth, very wrong. You can't do that with her around here. Or anywhere…it's not right and people don't understand. I'm afraid you'll get hurt. You can't be telling Fort over the loudspeaker that you love her and want to marry her. People don't understand. You can tell her in private only. Okay?"

"Ms. Tomlinson?" A voice from across the gym. I looked over my shoulder. It was Malone. She had Melissa Fortunata with her. Fortunata dragged her sneakers across the floor and they squeaked and echoed in the dusty gym's haze and glare.

"Hey, Ms. Malone? Who's got your class?" I asked.

"Mrs. Selden has covered my class for a few minutes."

Then Fortunata broke from her and lumbered ecstatically over to Cichetti. She held her hands out with the frog Cichetti had given her the day before in them, and Cichetti took it and smiled. Flip.

"Are they passing frog money?" I jabbed.

Malone rolled her eyes at me. "It's their way of showing love to one another. Don't you teach English and write poetry?" The double doors slammed and the four of us stood on the gym floor holding court.

"Now, Malone, that's hitting below the belt. You're much better at this than I am. I quit. I can't keep up with Cichetti and her shenanigans." I ran my hands through my hair as Cichetti and Fortunata began passing the ball back and forth.

Malone came up to me and we stood face to face. She put her hands on her round hips, militant-like. "Carrie, you can't quit on them. You—and me—we're all on the same team. My whole class, including Fortunata, went beserk when Elizabeth asked her to marry her. Just on the way down here, I heard a bunch of kids talking about it in the art room. They were on the sidewalk and they actually sounded okay with it. Hello, it's 2009; are you still in 1984?"

"I'm still with Susan and I can't think beyond anything but her." I turned and slapped the wall. My eyes burned with fire. "Malone, Malone, Malone. What am I going to do with all of you?" I turned around and faced her again. The clock said nine ten.

Cichetti twiddled her hands in the air and Fortunata did the same. Two retarded girls in love. Jesus Christ. What in heaven's sake was going on?

"What are they doing now?" I asked. "I think I just broke my hand."

"Mimicking one another. They love to do it." Malone went over and grabbed the ball. "You're going to have to let them do this, Carrie. It's okay for a Down Syndrome girl to like another girl of her likeness. It happens. Happens all the time whether we like it or not. They have the same feelings we do."

I held my hand and rubbed it. "Yeah, but I'm getting flack from all over. Students...now parents. What am I supposed to do? I could lose half my team over this and can't we lose our jobs by starting a GSA? I want out...do retarded people do it?"

"Carrie, shut up. You're the retard! I swear sometimes I should just bring River up to your house and sic her on you. It's the kids who want to start the GSA. That's what makes it okay. And, since when did you care about any of this?"

"I don't care, Malone. I just don't feel like it's okay for a DS kid to ask an EMR kid to marry her over the loudspeaker. They're seniors in high school for God's sake."

Malone turned and shuffled toward me, two inches from my face. Rosy. Her cheeks were turning rosy.

"They're both twenty-one and will be graduating together this year. It's their last year of eligibility."

I walked over to Fortunata and Cichetti. Fortunata was sticking her tongue out at Cichetti and then they spontaneously

63

hugged each other and then me. Both of them around my legs. Fort on one side and Cichetti on the other. Holy cow!

"Frog," Fortunata said to me. She looked up at me and put the frog in my hand, her frizzy hair higher than usual. Just a day earlier, she'd been stuck in a bathroom with urine in her hair. Now, she was handing me my lime green plastic flippy frog Cichetti had taken from me.

"Frog," I repeated back.

Cichetti grabbed my hand and closed the frog into it. I cocked my head to the right. "Fort wants you to have it, Mith Tomlinthon."

Oh, the circle of love. I was getting my frog back.

"Why?" I asked. Fort remained quiet and Cichetti just shrugged.

"I tell you what," I said. "I'll keep it on my windowsill at home and every time I look at it, I will think of you two. Okay? Now let's get to class and just worry about what we're having for lunch the rest of the morning."

Malone walked up and grabbed Fort's hand. "What are we having for lunch Fort?" she asked.

"Chicken nuggetth!" Cichetti punched both hands up in the air.

"Yes." Fort said and gently smiled her head down.

Then Cichetti hugged Fort, a solid embrace punctuated by a sway. Slowly, our small court affair was dismissed into the rest of the infernal day.

Only later, we would find out that yes meant Fort wanted to marry Elizabeth Cichetti.

# Chapter 7

Eddie Cichetti and Annie Cichetti were fuming mad that things had gotten away from the teachers and administration at Sterling Road High School. This was the last thing I heard from Principal Snod-ass prior to catching the bus to Albemarle High School for our first basketball game of the season. They wanted a meeting with me and Malone and the staff responsible for Cichetti and also wanted Fortunata's parents contacted. Apparently, Eddie was in charge of the Cichetti household and he wanted answers to why things had escalated in such a short amount of time. Snod-ass bent my ear all the way to, and as we got on, the bus. Malone was there and reminded me to keep my eye on you-know-who.

Halloween was around the corner and the ghastliness of it all was plucking the three nerves I had left. We showed up, my team played terribly, and I longed for a twelve-pack of Miller Lite to assuage and expunge the hole that was growing larger inside of me. The pick-and-roll offense we'd practiced with Robin and Juanita was capital. Six times Juanita picked on the wrong man, usually she picked one of her own teammates to pick because her nerves had gotten the best of her. Then Terri Boisseau showed her nerves by giving up the ball on eight of her own turnovers. Six of the turnovers turned into points for Albemarle. After we lost the game by seventeen points, the remaining two nerves were being uprooted by none other than ELIZABETH CICHETTI. Lost again. Lost, lost, lost.

Cichetti kept the team from getting back to school because she had somehow noodled her Down Syndrome way all the way to the administrative wing of Albemarle High School (how she had gotten there no one knew). Looking for another microphone to be heard, Cichetti was drawn once again to the loudspeaker. Upon turning around the corner to the admin wing, I found her twiddling her arms and jumping up and down.

"Elizabeth Cichetti!" I barked. I was boiling and bounced up to her. "You need to get on the bus so we can all get home asap! How did you get here?" I threw my clipboard down and unzipped my nylon SRHS jacket. "Answer me. How did you get here?"

No eye contact. She looked at her shoes.

"I want to make an announcement," she said matter-of-factly, peering through the glass of the administrative offices. A janitor pushed his cart from around the corner and began sweeping the front of the entranceway to the school.

"How did you get here? Never mind, that doesn't matter. The folks at this school have locked up for the day. Come on!" I grabbed her hand.

She shook it off and twiddled her hands in the air. Her white button-down shirt was still untucked from shooting earlier with the opposing team. I put my hands on my hips and watched the janitor sweep the leaves out the front door.

Pickle jogged up from behind me. "She gave the other team good luck, Coach T. She shot baskets with the entire Albemarle team during warm-ups and during halftime. Maybe we should suit her up and have her play with us?"

"Pickle. Shut it and help me out here." I'd had it with everyone.

"Another thing, Elliot Brisbane told Claire Austin who told Jack Ignatio that the GSA was going to back Cichetti and Fort up," Pickle stated, moving closer. "The GSA is going to back them up. It didn't sound dipple-matic."

I exhaled deeply. "Diplomatic, you mean. Come on Pick. Can you just help me get Cichetti off this hallway."

Pickle tried a few times but Cichetti stood her ground. Pickle said she would go and get Cichetti's dad.

"Fine. Hurry up!" Pickle picked up a jog around the corner.

I continued to try and get Cichetti away from the door, but she could see the microphone to their system on the counter. She just wanted to be heard. Something Malone would probably think. Malone. Malone. Malone. Always alone. The epitaph lesson needed a conclusion. Maybe I could write Malone's epitaph as a joke. Lighten up her spirits a bit.

When Eddie Cichetti rounded the corner five minutes later, his neatly cropped ebony-black buzz cut and neatly pressed shirt and tie exemplified the successful real estate developer he was. Right behind him was the demure, slightly shy wife and mother, Annie Cichetti. Her strawberry-blond hair was shoulder-length and pressed from a hot iron and her sweater was buttoned nearly to the top. Her large black purse was hanging at her elbow as if she'd jogged part way.

"Okay, Elizabeth. We've had quite the day now haven't we?" His disdain was apparently directed at the situation, not at her.

Annie Cichetti reached for Elizabeth. "Come on little one, let's go home. I've made some spaghetti—just the way you like it. It has cheddar cheese on top and we can eat it all up right away."

"I want to marry Fortunata, Mom. She likes my frog. Fortunata likes my frog."

"Well, this is a first." Eddie stepped closer and slid his hand down his tie. "She's more interested in Fortunata than a plate of her favorite food." He affectionately slapped me on the back.

"Elizabeth, I have the frog. Remember? You guys gave it to me?"

"Mith Tomlinthon, we can get another one and then we can get you a band like mine for your wrist. For luck. Fort and luck. Luck."

"Did you hear about the loudspeaker incident this morning?" I asked him, already knowing the answer. Pickle slowly backed up. I motioned with a nod for her to go on back to the bus.

"Annie told me. Mr. Snodgrass called to tell her that Elizabeth was making funnies over the loudspeaker. Hmm. Eh. Elizabeth. You hear me?"

Cichetti reached out and grabbed her mother's hand and grinned up at me. "Mith Tomlinthon, we scored tonight."

"Yes, Cichetti girl, we scored." And then under my breath, "Just not enough. We just didn't score enough."

Annie Cichetti in her quiet and delicate way was able to get Elizabeth away from the glass and guide her, holding her hand, back down to the gym. Eddie and I made small talk and he told me that Elizabeth had been twiddling with more excitement lately since she'd gotten closer to some of the other "retarded" girls—as he said it. I did not say much as I'd had it: Monday the prison bathroom break, and then a very loud modest proposal over the entire sound system of STERLING ROAD HIGH SCHOOL today. And now losing a season opener to a school we should have shut down in the first half. Now, with the father of the girl who was beginning to annoy the hell out of me. I must admit I did not understand how parents of exceptional ed students lived. How in the hell did they have a life? I only had Elizabeth Cichetti two maybe three hours a day. I couldn't imagine a lifetime. So, my nerves were gone and my shallowness surfaced. In my heart, I knew I couldn't do it. I was too interested in myself, my sex life and my booze. After a fairly ordinary day at SRHS the next day, I decided I needed a Charlotte and Sammie fix to get the cobwebs out of my head. I invited Malone along but did not tell her Sammie would be there. Secrets. We needed some more secrets. My thoughts needed to get off GSA's, Down Syndrome, non-verbal EMR students and on to something else. What that something else was, I wasn't quite sure

Immediately on arrival, Malone, still dressed in her khaki slacks and orange knit sweater she had worn to school, went to my kitchen sink and began to wash some dishes. My small bungalow was always unkempt and I liked it that way. The small cabin I had shared with Susan was in the middle of a sweeping vista of the Blue Ridge valley. The wood was eighty years old and the kitchen was small. A cook stove and a green Formica counter had bread crumbs and bills and pens scattered on top. The wooden floors were dusty and the old oriental rugs were in dire need of a vacuuming.

"Audra Malone, please don't wash my dishes. Really!" I charged up from behind her and grabbed her arm. I accidentally knocked over three of my hope stones and the plaster imprint of Scout's paw. Rearranging them back on the sill, I said, "I've got plenty of time on Saturday to wash them up. The pizza plates and beer bottles can wait."

"Sorry about your stones…here let me help you. Where are we meeting Charlotte?" she asked as she grabbed a hand towel that was due for the laundry and wiped off her hands. She had her hair up and scrutinized me in a funny way.

"What?" I asked and popped open a beer.

"You drink too much."

"You talk too much." I turned around and walked into the living room and stared through the bay window. "Since when did you become my mother?" I yelled into the kitchen.

She walked in and sat on the couch. "Since when did you forget we were best friends? Best friends tell each other things and I've known you for a long while and you drink way too much. It always gets you in trouble with women. Jesus, Carrie, how many women have you gotten drunk over?"

"I've lost count."

"God, we are polar opposites. You lose count and I can't even get in the top ten. Is it all that exciting to you?"

Ignoring that question, I said, "Why don't you put an ad in the paper or go to Match dot com. An ad might be a good idea."

Charlotte, dressed in tight jeans and an untucked blue shirt and vest, walked in the screen door just as I was giving Malone my newest ideas on how she could meet a woman.

"Why don't you two go out?" she challenged us. "You've known each other for years and love and hate each other at the same time. Don't most relationships end up that way anyway?" She put a bottle of pinot noir on the oak table that separated the living room from the kitchen and stretched out her legs. Charlotte: my brazen death buddy.

Malone flung herself into my La-Z-Boy chair. "How's the marathon training going and I would never be with Carrie Tomlinson because she's been defiled by half the women in the state of Virginia."

"I know." Charlotte looked at me.

I rolled my eyes and gave them both the finger.

"Have you infiltrated into any of the regional states, too?" Charlotte asked. "We best get to Green Top for our CAS as soon as we can so we don't hurt anyone else."

I walked to the kitchen to get another beer. When I cracked the beer open, I did it in Malone's face.

She waved her hands at me. "Get that beer out of my face. Did you know I talked at length with the GSAers today? All of them loved Elizabeth Cichetti's proclamation of love and plan on supporting her and Melissa Fortunata in a mock ceremony at the November dance."

"No, they won't!" I exclaimed. "Have you forgotten where we live? Let me remind you. The big, RED state of Virginia, you idiot savant. The faculty and parents, GSA or not, will have nothing to do with this fake nuptial and I'm, frankly, tired of the shenanigans of Elizabeth and Fortunata. I'm done with all of it."

"Fort said three more words today, Carrie."

Charlotte said, "That's good isn't it? I mean she doesn't talk much, right?"

"What were they?" I asked swallowing hard, clenching my teeth.

Malone ripped my beer from me and took a swallow. "She said, 'love, Malone' and 'finger.'"

"Love, Malone and finger," I repeated.

"Is she in love with your finger?" Charlotte asked incredulously.

"No, stupid. She said my name because I asked her for the eighty-seventh billionth time. As you might say, Carrie: you know billionth…" She stuck her tongue out at me. "Then she said love and finger—when she said this, she held her left hand."

"I am going to throw up!" I proclaimed and sat on my leather sofa, pulling my knees to me.

"Fine, throw up. I think it's cute and adorable that she and Elizabeth are in love and hope that on some level they can do what they want to do!"

"What's that? Get married? Are you kidding Malone? They are both mentally retarded and Melissa can't even say a whole sentence." I released my legs and arched my head back and closed my eyes. Jesus. This is bedlam.

Charlotte poured some wine and looked at us both like we were at a tennis match. Back and forth and back and forth. "Aww. Not even a whole sentence. That's so sad!"

"Don't feel sorry for her, Charlotte. She's doing really well. It's her parents I'm worried about. They may have to give her up because the mom is now sick and the father is too incapacitated himself. I'm going to make an early application to the Charlottesville Home to see if they can take her. I take River there every weekend to visit the residents." Malone retreated to the kitchen to get a Coke. I thought her hair might catch fire from her own driving thoughts. Did she ever think about anything but school and these kids?

"You don't get enough during the week? I didn't know you took River there. Oh! That's right, you did tell me. You got her to be a certified Delta Therapy Dog. I forgot," I said trying to make a bit of peace.

"Yes. You are forgetful. I thought poets and English teachers were supposed to have good memories, you know recite lines of love poems and all. I've never heard you recite anything, Carrie, except for how a four and five basketball player are supposed to post up." She sat down opposite me and swigged her Coke then made a minor face like *ha, ha*.

"How about the 'Lake Isle of Innisfree' by William Butler Yeats? Have you heard of that one, Malone?"

Malone gazed at me. "Don't tell me you know a poem by heart?"

Charlotte repeated the word Innisfree under her breath.

"I don't know anything about William Butler Yeats, Carrie, I teach exceptional ed"

"Sit up girls and listen…" I began. 'The Lake Isle of Innisfree' by William Butler Yeats.

*"I will arise and go now, and go to Innisfree, And a small cabin build there, of clay and wattles made: Nine bean-rows will I have there, a hive for the honey-bee And live alone in the bee-loud glade.*

*And I shall have some peace there, for peace comes dropping slow Dropping from the veils of the morning to where the cricket sings; There midnight's all a glimmer, and noon a purple glow, And evening full of the linnet's wings.*

*I will arise and go now, for always night and day I hear lake water lapping with low sounds by the shore; While I stand on the roadway, or on the pavements grey, I hear it in the deep heart's core."*

Malone and Charlotte were sitting like petrified trees. Neither moved.

Finally, Malone chimed in. "It's spectacular. Do it again…"

"No, I'm not doing it again." I slumped down.

Then it happened.

Suddenly, like the roof of my small home opened up channeling an evanescent light through a dark crystalline chasm—an angel appeared in the dusk of the October sky, the October night: a shift. I saw Malone in a different light—an angelic specter. A silent alarm went off in my body; a chill went up my spine; a rapturous grab in between my legs. The bright, funny exceptional ed teacher who had been my friend for a thousand years became attractive, sexual even. Slowly, I got up and went into the kitchen as I heard Malone and Charlotte make idle chit-chat. I peered at my windowsill—something I'd looked at everyday for years—at the frog and then the stones I'd gotten from the brook behind the school. Some stones had words on them: *love, dance, peace*. And there was a picture of Susan—the love of my life—with words and religious prayers from her funeral four years earlier. I went back to the living room swigging my beer.

I studied Malone. Her eyes were pinched inward. They were blue, almost icy. Her body was fit and slightly pear-shaped and she was short and her hair was similar to that of Fortunata's but she managed to have some control over it. It was gray by her temples near her perfectly shaped ears. I stood there in the area between the kitchen and the living room. I felt it again in my spine and between my legs. Whoosh. I looked back to the picture of Susan and then walked into the kitchen ignoring the nattering conversation that ensued. Charlotte kept mumbling the word Innisfree and asked Malone what it meant again. I did not pay attention. I was riveted on the picture of Susan. So, I went there and stood and stared at it. Susan. Susan. Susan. What are you doing?

Finally, after three centuries passed, Charlotte came in. "Well, Carrie, what does it mean?"

"What does what mean?" I asked back.

"Innisfree, stupid. Where have you been?"

Malone stepped in and repeated. "Yeah, Innisfree. What does it mean?"

I swallowed some beer for courage and glanced back at Susan and then patted the frog on the head. When I turned around, I wiped a tear that had bubbled from my eye. "It's about home. It's about going home." I covered my heart with my hands.

"Oh, honey. Are you sad about Susan?" Malone asked.

"No, I'm sad about me."

73

Charlotte stepped closer. "Oh, honey if you don't know the answer, we can Google it. Googling makes the whole world go around. We can find out what Innisfree means."

I snorted. "Home. It's Yeats home. The beauty of it is that he hears it in the deep heart's core. He wrote the poem when he was away from home. It's about longing."

Malone put her warm strong hand on my shoulder. "Do you need some sex to help you get through this? We can go down to Ray's and see if you can pick up a chick."

"Shut up." I wiped my tear with the back of my hand and laughed. Audra put her hand on my back. We smiled at one another momentarily. This time it was different. The hole in my soul felt different.

Just then, Sammie knocked on my door.

"Hey, Sammie. Thank God you are here. We were just getting into a huge discussion about the Charlottesville Home and poetry." Charlotte bounded to the door to help Sammie in. "It's a deep discussion."

"Oh." She walked in dressed in her produce uniform handling a twelve-pack and a bouquet of flowers. I looked at her, another weird behavior, then grabbed both of them from her. "I know that place. I deliver there once a week to the cafeteria. They are a standing order."

"Audra Malone. This is Sammie. Our local produce deliverer and two-step extraordinaire. If you ever came to Ray's, you would know this. I'm surprised you guys haven't met already seein's how we only have fourteen or fifteen lesbians in town plus the college kids." I said this and put the flowers in a vase. When Charlotte saw that I was having trouble fixing an appropriate arrangement she butt-hipped me out of the way and took over.

"You are so smart in some ways and so retarded in others," Charlotte quipped at me. "I'm going to kill you," she said and winked at me.

I laughed and said, "Careful saying the word 'retarded' around Malone. She may cease and desist from talking to any one of us."

Sammie paid no attention and in her nervousness to meet Malone kept talking about The Charlottesville Home. "The people there have mental and physical disabilities and they are a self-serving community, like. They have service dogs and a huge staff. The staff that work in the cafeteria are always very nice and they teach the residents how to load and unload from my truck. It's kind of cool, like."

"I think we should get Fortunata in this place after she graduates," Malone said.

"Maybe she and Elizabeth could live there happily ever after." I stomped down the hall to the bathroom. When I re-emerged, everyone was sitting in the living room.

Sammie was talking about some tunnel in Richmond that had people trapped in it from 1926.

"Sammie, what are you talking about?" I asked.

She was sitting next to Malone and I did not at all like it for a reason whose definition I could not muster up. I liked Malone single and my best friend. I did not want anything to happen between her and Sammie. So, I plopped down in between them and smacked Malone on the thigh. Charlotte gave me the look of death, so I got up and moved over to her side, sitting on a large leather oversized chair and crossing my feet hard on the ottoman.

Sammie talked on with her large veiny hands a-wavering around and took her cap off in mid-sentence to reveal some gray-brown tufts. "I deliver to Richmond sometimes and there's this really cool train wreck that happened back in like 1926. It was coming through a hill in Church Hill and as it did, the ground and everything just collapsed all around the train. The people are still in there. They couldn't get them out, like."

"Like, how do you know this?" I asked, leaning over to turn on my floor lamp.

"Sammie, that's really cool." Charlotte smacked me with a look of disgust.

Malone shifted in her seat. "So, it's a tomb? Is the tunnel capped?"

Sammie gazed at Malone. I suddenly wanted to throw up. Sammie swallowed her beer and nodded. "Yeah, like it's got a cement structure all around the tunnel's entrance and it's only stamped with the number 1926. Like, that's it. It's behind the cold storage building. It seems like barely anyone knows about it. Every time I'm there, I look at it and can't imagine how those people felt having a tunnel collapse on them on their way to Richmond."

"It sucked, like," I chimed in. "That's what it felt like and now they are entombed in that place. Feels creepy to me."

"Feels crappy to me," Charlotte said.

"Well, I'm hungry." Malone crossed then re-crossed her legs and looked right at me.

God, she's hungry. My gape back at her stayed still for a moment—holding, holding, holding. Then, she looked at Sammie who did not return her glance.

Tired from the poetry and tunnel dynamics and my new burgeoning dynamic for Malone, I decided I did not want to go anywhere. "Why don't you guys go to Ray's or wherever. I'll see you tomorrow at school, Malone, and then maybe all four of us could do coffee on Saturday morning after my big Friday game."

"Who are you playing?"

"Lynchburg High School. Home. If I can keep Cichetti from flying out of the bus trying to find a karaoke machine or a microphone, it will be a good night. Her mother told us that after the Albemarle incident they'd bought Cichetti a karaoke machine for her birthday last August. Annie said she played with it practically every night. She sings John Denver's 'Sunshine On My Shoulders' all the time. Ahh. John Denver."

Cichetti, from what I learned that night, had a penchant for listening to her own voice.

Now, as it were, I had a penchant for Audra Malone.

God works in mysterious ways.

# Chapter 8

Before I left my house on Thursday, I put my stained coffee mug in the stained sink and placed on the windowsill a new rock that Sammie had given me. She had a penchant for collecting them with certain words like *grace, wit, wisdom.* So, I placed it all there on my windowsill like a shrine of belief and melancholy. Especially with Susan's picture adorning the middle. I peered through the window at the ancient swing that hung off the oak tree in my backyard. Scanning the grass for a moment, I went back to the night before when I'd thought of Malone. How weird? Why was I suddenly attracted to my best friend? I had my own suspicious thoughts. Could I kiss her? Would she even want to kiss me after all that she knew about me and all these years? What was I thinking!

I can't be attracted to her. Oy vay. I'm not even Jewish. Why the hell am I thinking that? I mumbled to myself, "Malone,

Malone, Malone…"

Maybe I just needed a puppy.

The October air smelled of hay and dew and humidity exhaled from the long summer of moist, ninety degree compression on Charlottesville.

When I arrived at school, I got out of my rickety Jeep Cherokee hooptie as Pickle called it and clamored for my portfolio prop. Holding a Styrofoam cup of coffee in my mouth, I walked precariously into the office. I saw Elizabeth sitting slumped and smelling like eggs at the intercom. Just staring at it. Gazing at it. Loving it. She barely looked up at me.

Peggy Schindler and I locked eyes. She rolled her eyes and I rolled mine. Here, she summoned me over with a finger and leaned into me. Sipping my coffee, I leaned back. My brain was fuzzy from too many beers and my mouth was cotton dry.

"I think some of the kids you have in your fifth period have done some bad stuff again." She looked around the office to see if anyone was listening. I did the perimeter check with her.

She went on. "Mr. Snodgrass and I came in early this morning and there was some graffiti on the wall around building nine. It said, *retarded dykes and fags go home*."

"No," I said incredulously.

"Yeah," she stated. "The janitors are fixing it right now with some chemicals and paint. But, if you ask me…" She leaned in closer, "If you ask me, those kids in the GSA need to be on the lookout and help those girls."

Malone sauntered in right behind me and asked, "Don't you think the faculty should be on the lookout and help those girls?" Then she looked at us with an expectant expression. She still wore a pumpkin pin just above her small breast.

I jolted up. "Jesus Christ, Malone. You scared the hell out of me."

"Well, if Jesus Christ and hell need to be summoned to get your attention, then maybe we can have a séance later and get you all fixed up. Watch your mouth, by the way, you know you can't say hell in school," she mocked me then patted me on the back, then walked over to Cichetti.

"Come on, honey. I think we can wait till next week to begin our lunch announcements again. Let's go to class and you and Fort can do some organizing for me."

Cichetti glanced at me. "Take away…" Three times she said this as she and Malone locked hands.

Neither one of them said a word. Two walking conundrums. Complex with different IQs. "See you at lunch duty!" I said loudly and then felt stupid for doing it. Stupid. Stupid. Stupid. Malone turned and looked at me but still did not say a word. I was getting it that she was perturbed with me. Not at my actions. My inaction.

Something felt wrong and out of place—off kilter. Cichetti should be reading the lunch announcements. My team was playing worse than any team I'd coached in nearly ten years and my fifth-period class was holding hostages of hate with spray paint on the walls of building nine and urinating on a mute's head. Fortunata. They had peed all over her head. What else had they done?

I grabbed my mail and blankly nodded to three teachers. I walked through the maelstrom of messages and guidance counselors and morning mayhem in the main office toward my room. I glanced down the walkway to where the custodians were cleaning up the graffiti of hate and ignorance. It smelled of alcohol, solvent and Clorox. That's right, bleach the shit out. Holy crap.

I've never been very religious. I've mainly tampered like a locksmith in the Catholic and Methodist schools of religious thinking. I remain still the world's worst Catholic except in the categories of guilt and humiliation and now stupidity. But, my vision began to unveil itself like it had the night before—I began to see, slowly, unhurriedly…I did not like any of it. Revelation: Carrie Tomlinson.

Pupils and teachers were milling about, trudging up and down the walkways oblivious yet subconsciously observant that I was among them. I, the alien, was dressed like them, the other teachers. White cotton shirt, pleated pants, silver earrings, silver beaded necklace. My dark brown wedged loafers were buckled. My head became unleashed. Begin. Now. A Voice in my head. Begin. Now. Go… Go… Go. Okay, I was not on some psychotic break. What in the world was inside of me? Who were these people…?

Wiggers (as they called themselves) and grunge heads, bespeckled in flannel and leather and silver studs, cloistered and hovered around one another dealing out their bits of wisdom on bands, guitars and lyrics to metallic songs. The jocks and the cheerleaders huddled around the walkways and thought about SAT scores, UVA, and whose parents were going out of town and did you, by the way, study for the English quiz? A few well-dressed teachers from the fashionable West End of Charlottesville sprang to and fro and chatted about tests, and computers and which winery they were going to this weekend. Teachers who had taught too long echoed some of the same sentiments as the grunge heads did, their eyes, these seasoned teachers, were tired and red from either too much grading or too much alcohol or a combination of the two. Coaches bantered about in their own clique discussing scores over hot coffee. They were staring away from me but in the same moment at me with their bulbous eyes. Like hot irons running through me, I felt the energy of what they were thinking. I was the other gay one like Malone. What girls' basketball coach wasn't gay? We had a corner on the market.

Suddenly, I was jaded, sullied. Green around the gills, sick to my stomach, I wanted to run away from this place as the eyes were now all over me. I wanted to retreat back to my car and fly home and wash dishes and look out my window and study the mystical ways melancholy gripped me, held me, made love to me. Jesus. Who was I kidding? I wasn't a poet. I just wanted to go home. William Damn Butler Yeats. Innisfree. Home. In my deep heart's core.

My head was still abuzz with this futile plea as I ventured into building nine and with a bit of disrespect for everything sauntered into my classroom. Room 103. I spent my entire planning period staring out the window onto Sterling Road thinking of how to run away, get out of this place, drop teaching, drop basketball, run away. I wanted everything, including the world, to go away. Except, for some dumb reason: Audra Malone.

So, what does she do? Malone skips lunch duty. So I held the line crashers at bay and ate at the front table by myself, nodding to students and players when they looked my way.

When my fifth period came in after lunch, I looked up from my podium as my students coolly jagged in. Their eyes studied me as usual, like, "Who the hell are you?"

And, then I think it was Tulio Grayson who murmured the indecipherable, "Enow."

Jack Ignatio followed with his version, "E-e-e-e-N-a-a-u-g-h."

Then a young one from the back did the same as Tulio. "Enow."

*What in the world was this*, I thought.

Then a few seconds later, half the class was just saying, "E-e-e!" and fairly loudly.

"Okay," I said. "What's with the e-e-e-n-o-w?" I asked. E-e-e's began like a shrilling band of choristers throughout the class and each of the boy students got up and almost yelled it like a enow mantra.

"Down, you e-e-er's," I said, "down." They eventually settled down. Like a freakin' uprising in the middle of the day.

"Poetry recitations are due today," I said. Then a squeaky e-e-e-n-o-w from the back in the last of the revolt came.

Glancing at my lime green walls, I studied the American greats lining my walls: Emerson, Thoreau, Fitzgerald, Hemingway. Their eyes were far away, musty from years of yellowing from the sun that emanated through the two windows in the room. The classroom's desks were clustered in two directions: one cluster facing the other with a walkway in the middle which directed to my small teacher's desk. The podium I stood behind: a small skeleton, a tripod connected to a piece of slanting wood. In my enow misery, I could not find solace or respite behind it. There were no hiding places here.

Unless, you were locked in a bathroom.

"Jack Ignatio, you're up first," I stated and peered at him. He was halfway down in his seat and fiddled with a piece of paper.

"Which poet are you doing?" I marked a check by his name.

He looked at me like I had three heads. "Where are you going to sit?"

He waited about five seconds and said, "Enow. No."

"Tomorrow?" I asked.

"Enow. Yes," he said.

By the seventh student, I had one who was ready. A ten-line recitation was all it was and they could pick any poet, modern or not, they wanted. It was Chandler Stevenson and he was ready.

"Which poem? Hand me the copy," I stated.

He walked up to my desk nervously. Chandler was a football player and was usually busting up; but he was fairly concerned with his grades since it was football season.

From the back of the room, "E-E-E…"

It was starting to piss me off but I held my composure.

Chandler handed me the poem. "Oh, I see," I said, "this is a good one. I like—"

Tulio stood up. "E-e-e-N-a-u-g-h."

My hair split. "Okay, what is it with this new incarnation of enow's or enaugh's? What's the beef, people?" I looked at Sherry Proffitt who I thought might give me some reason but she looked down in embarrassment that I'd even looked at her because looking at her meant she was alive and she didn't want to be. And, at this particular moment, I understood her plight.

Chandler bumbled through one of the shortest poems in American literature. "Plums" by William Carlos Williams. Talk about a redundant name. I never knew why anyone liked the poem. Was it just because there were no other good plum poems? No one had written about that fruit?

I gave him three prompts as the E-E-Es continued from around the room. I looked out the window and stopped listening for a moment and peered at Sterling Road. I wanted to be out there on the road and away from the dismal days of Down

Syndrome and retarded lesbian lovers and onto the pathway of wherever any of those cars might go.

"Ms. Tomlinson?" Chandler was in front of me. "How'd I do?"

"You suck!" came Tulio's retort. The dark Gothic shit that he was.

I stood up. "Tulio, give it a break for one day. Can you?"

He did not respond.

In my misery, I thought again of Malone and her whisking Elizabeth away and skipping our lunch duty together.

"You were adequate, Chandler, thank you." He squinched his eyes at me.

This class was abysmal.

"Next?" I asked. No one looked at me and I settled into doodling for a moment on the punctuation tests in front of me. I didn't care either. And, now, of course, this was another problem.

We sat in silence for twenty long minutes before I asked Sherry Proffitt if she wanted to go. She shrugged and I asked her if she was ready. She eked out "Tomorrow" and I said that that would be fine.

The grace of God—the bell rang and the enowers left my room. I went to the door with vocabulary quizzes in hand to police the hall and saw Cichetti with Fortunata by her side, almost huddled near the lockers as they ambled along. I looked down at my quizzes and began to grade them. Out of the corner of my eye, I saw Jack Ignatio lean against the wall in his ripped jeans and black T-shirt while he scanned the crowd of students moving like cattle through the concrete hallway. Tulio Grayson came jagging confidently from around the corner with his shaved head and tattoos and I noticed them discussing something. Down I looked and graded the next paper and waved at Cichetti and Fortunata as they passed by me on their way back to Malone's class after Art I with Mrs. Mary, as they called her.

Then, as the students were disappearing into their classrooms, Vivian Johnson and Claire Austin came down the hallway. Elliot Brisbane, who had refound his mohawk, which was standing on end, followed three feet behind them holding his man purse and swaggering a bit.

Pivotal. It was so pivotal, I didn't even see it coming.

Elliot yelled that Jack Ignatio wanted to suck cock more than Tulio Grayson. It was so loud that I was sure that Snodgrass and all the secretaries in the admin building could hear it. It re-echoed and slowed the space of time and travel to a standstill.

Claire yelled, "Closet fags. Have to lock a girl in the bathroom to feel how powerful you are. And—"

Vivian grabbed Claire's hand. "Why don't you lock us up? Huh? Come on. Make your brass balls brass, you—"

Tulio and Jack bristled and came forward.

I watched.

Cichetti and Fortunata, feeling the arcing wave of weird energy, moved closer to the lockers and looked back at me, almost in unison. Then I looked at them and noticed that Cichetti grabbed Fortunata's hand as she began to get agitated and twiddle her hands in the air. They cowered. I watched. My feet were pinned to the floor. Looking back down at the quizzes, I hoped for another teacher to arrive.

Vivian and Claire stood face-to-face with Jack and Tulio and then I saw Thunder Bucknell come down the hallway from the other direction.

It was all planned.

The text messages on the cell phones must have been hot since the bathroom incident, and the enclaves of liberal students and their own philosophies on how people should be treated were zeroed in on by the insular, provincial thinking kids who didn't know the Bible but used it as a weapon anyway.

"Fuck you!" Tulio said to the girls. "You cunt-lickin' skanks. I'll show you some dick." He grabbed his crotch.

"Yeah." Jack imitated Tulio. "I've got enough here to make you want to cry out for more. You just haven't had enough of my cock in you. Are you still a virgin? Most lesbians are till they've had this. Come on. We'll take you to the bathroom and show you how it's done."

It gave him away. Was Melissa Fortunata raped? I shook it from my head and continued to stare.

Just then, Jack reached around to the back of Vivian's head and grabbed her hair. Claire shoved him out of the way and Jack teetered into Tulio which put him off balance. Thunder Bucknell tackled them both to the ground and then the anarchy devised from the texting came alive. Three black girls came in and started shouting and hitting each other.

It was fuck you this and fuck you that.

I stared.

Then I dropped my pen and papers to the floor. Three teachers from around the corner came in to break up the mélange of rednecks, fags, dykes, wiggers, posers, whatevers and the alarm sounded. Melody Roane had hit her classroom alarm. She was my teaching neighbor and rarely came out to monitor the hallway like me.

Unraveling. It was an unraveling. Cichetti and Fortunata came back toward me during the fight and I told them to go the other way. Take the long way to Malone's room I had told them. It was the only good thing I did in the middle of the biggest fight I'd ever seen.

Anchored to the floor as Snodgrass and a vice principal appeared, I finally managed to lean down and pick up my pen and papers and step and stare blankly back into my room. I simply and without care walked into my classroom where Innisfree lit up the room with glowing stars. The lights were out. The two windows that opened to the road were lit up.

E-e-e-n-o-w. It was echoing in my ears from my fifth-period class.

In the dark, I grabbed a dictionary from my desk to find this word I did not know. Enow. Enow. Enow.

Enow, I traced my finger down the e's to find the n then the o. It was an archaic word. I read the etymology, then the definition.

It meant enough. Enow meant enough.

Enow.

# Chapter 9

Driving away from Sterling Road High School that day, I went directly to the store next to Charlotte's favorite pizza parlor and bought a twelve-pack of Miller Lite and drove halfway to Middleburg thinking and trying to figure out what was going on with me, my teaching, my coaching and my love interests. Before, I had control over my classes. Before, I had won games and enjoyed practice. Before, I had been always on someone's arm down at Ray's drinking my face off and going home to have drunken sex. Before, my life was easy. Teach. Coach. Sex. The order in which I liked it.

Now, everything was awry. Ever since Cichetti had made her marriage proposal the school's foundation had cracked and everyone was triggered into behaving like it was anarchy 101. I felt like Roderick Usher in Poe's *Fall of the House of Usher*. Like him, I was entombed in my own thinking. His sister entombed in a mock grave inside the house. All of the senses going into overdrive: the faintest ray of light too much to see; a simple violin chord too much to hear; clothes hanging on the skin too much to feel. His home and family having all of its ties severed and his childhood friend who comes to help witnesses the demise as the house and the people inside come crashing down. Bleak damn story. Sterling Road High School was falling apart and so was I. I just wanted things back to how they had been.

Looking out the window of my beat-up Grand Cherokee, I watched the rolling hills of the low lying mountains of the Blue Ridge rise and fall. The bucolic fields and fence-line instilled a kind of pathos, a longing in me that I did not know was there. I drained my third beer and turned the country music off. Drifting to the desert the Eagles were just singing about. Something about making love in the desert, under the orange moon, maybe? Ah, me. The moon. Twilight on these roads and I opened beer four and put it between my legs.

I went to Susan. Her memory faded like the way time travels and you can't catch it as much as you want to: to hold on to a memory, a picture, still and alluring in your head. I swallowed long and hard to rub away the pain that heaved into my chest. I thought of her and was pissed off that she'd left me in this life without her. Left alone to bear life without her was like being a captive in a realm you wanted no part of. I wanted no part of this stupidity any longer.

Boy, was I getting dark and depressed. I needed to call someone. Charlotte? Sammie? Malone? Fumbling for my cell phone, I accidentally spilled my beer onto the floorboard. Crap. When the blue lights came on behind me, I could not remember the speed at which I was going. Now, I really wanted to be a character in some dumb story about a house crumbling down.

I pulled over on the side of the road. Quickly, I fumbled for a penny. Numerous times, I heard in my head—get a penny in your mouth. I pulled my sock off and threw it over the spilled beer and found only nickels to put in my mouth. Three. Was I drunk or just buzzed?

Checking the rearview mirror, I saw the officer get out of his car. I tried checking his countenance: serious. It looked very serious, very serious. He looked like a uniformed teenager.

I scrambled to get out my license and registration. When I opened the glove box, the lever gave way and the whole bottom half fell on the floorboard of the passenger side. Papers and matches and two bottle openers strewn all over the passenger's side.

Rolling my window down, I managed to shift the nickels to the right side of my mouth. The night was as dark as his uniform and the lights from his patrol car kept reflecting on me through my rearview mirror. The lights whirred around and around.

"Evenin', ma'am." The officer was behind my direct line of vision, off to the side.

"Evenin', Orthifer, wha' did I do wrung?" I wiped my mouth and shifted the nickels back to my rear molars.

"Well, tell me how fast you think you were going?" he asked.

"Thixty-three or fo'." I swallowed, one nickel down. Two to go.

"Well, I clocked you going seventy-eight in a sixty mile an hour zone. Can I see your ID and registration?" He pulled his belt up and stuck his thumb in on one side.

"Shore," I handed them over and then looked at myself in the mirror. Red eyes. I looked like a chipmunk and my cartoon heart was beating clear through my chest. The lights whirred again and again.

"I smell alcohol," he said.

"You thmell," I swallowed number two, "owlcohol?"

"Yes, ma'am. Have you been drinking?"

I never lied. "Well, orthifer," I swallowed the third and wiped my mouth again, "to tell you the truth, I have had a few…"

"Say your ABC's from A to P," he told me.

I was lucky I taught English. When I started, no problem. Then, I stumbled over the L-M-N-O part. It sounded more like Helen Hunt. Freudian skirt. Here, he asked me to step out of the car. He said something in his walkie on his shoulder and before I knew it, there was another policeman with his blue lights flashing. I was in the middle of Greene County. It was nearly seven p.m. on a cool October night and the moon in all of its orbit-like intuition cascaded a yellowing light over the series of Olympic events I had to do in order to pass the drunk test: there was Balance Beam with One Leg Up. I scored a three. There was Find Your Nose using the tips of your index fingers. I scored a 2.5 from the second Greene County officer because I went for my teeth and chin. Then there was the Blow in This Tube to see what my lung capacity was. I scored a .10.

"You're under arrest," said the initial officer. He read me my rights and then handcuffed me and put me in the front seat of his car.

I thought I would throw up. I could lose my job. This was serious. Help me Susan. Help me. I was going to jail.

All the way to jail, I stared straight ahead, stoic. I breathed heavily and thought I might cry. But, I held it in. I wasn't a crier and wasn't about to become one. The officer asked me more questions but I did not answer because even though I was buzzed, I had wits enough to know to keep silent. Stay silent and no one will know what you did, who you are, blah, blah, blah. In more ways than one.

When we got to the Greene County jail, I was taken to the intake section where I was released from the cuffs and asked to remove everything from my being: necklace, wallet, checkbook, and a ring that Susan had given me that I wore on my right hand.

"Can I make a phone call?" I asked the intake officer who stood leaning against the counter and talking to the female officer behind him. My words fell on deaf ears.

So, I asked again. "Can I make a phone call?" Nothing again.

The female officer moved forward and stood next to her buddy. "Did you get all the personal items?"

The officer pushed his glasses up and sighed loudly, "All but that ring on her finger."

The female officer looked at me. "We're going to need everything removed. It's a part of intake here."

"Who do I need to speak to to get a phone call?" I asked, pulling the ring from my hand and placing it delicately on the counter. She swooped it up and put it in a baggy.

Her cohort chimed in. "You have to see the magistrate first. Once you see the magistrate, then you can make your phone call. Now, we need you to step into this room so you can get your picture taken."

Mugshot. I could not believe I was in jail. I needed a substitute for tomorrow. I'd never been to jail. When they asked me to turn from side to side for my pictures, I felt as low as low could be. Fifth period was low; but, this was lower.

Then came the stupid games where you jump through hoops. All I wanted was a phone call. After the photo shoot came your medical exam. I'd never heard of such a thing. I was walked by an officer to medical intake where they filled out paperwork for all inmates. There was an African American lady sitting at a metal desk piled with papers who asked me a series of questions. She looked like she hated her job and she gave me a small bit of hope when she smiled at me.

"What is your religion?" she asked as she went down the list of questions.

I shifted in my seat—I'd thought of this earlier in the day. "What? Why does that matter?"

She looked down her nose at me. "Just something on the form we gotta ask. You gonna answer or do I need to call Carleen over?"

I didn't know who Carleen was but decided to give in. "Pagan," I said with certainty of no salvation from this place.

Carefully and with large letters, she wrote in PAGAN. Then there were questions about family medical history: heart disease, diabetes, mental illness. I stopped her at mental illness and said, "Yes. My uncle had OCD."

She wrote in large letters out to the side: OCD.

"He's especially good at arranging spices in alphabetical order. Can you put that in there?"

She looked at me, then over her shoulder yelled, "Carleen! This one's ready for you."

"Can I get my phone call?"

"Carleen's going to do that for you after you see the magistrate. What are you in here for anyway?" she asked.

"DUI," I said. "You can put that by OCD or something. I guess I've got an alcohol compulsion."

Carleen was the biggest redneck officer I'd seen. She came over with a pockmarked face and flimsy, stringy hair and her belly was hanging over her belt. She leaned forward when she walked like she had to get there with her head first to make an impression.

"I've got you now," she said with enthusiasm. "You ain't gonna give me no trouble now, are you?" She asked this then recuffed me. With Carleen as my dyke-in-uniform escort, she led me down the hallway back to a room where my arresting officer was writing up his report on me. The hallway smelled like body odor and the institutional white on the hallway walls was chipped and scuffed at the bottom.

"You need her anymore, Martin?" Carleen yelled through the doorway.

"Nah, we made her blow in the field and then once in the tank here. She's not saying anything till she's got a lawyer. Is that right?" He looked at me.

"Just want to make that phone call," I said, looking at him then to Carleen. It was beginning to occur to me that even though I was in jail around a bunch of officers who supposedly upheld the law, I had truly lost all my rights. I was cuffed and with Carleen and it felt creepy and weird and hopeless. All of my jewelry was in some baggy somewhere. I was praying for a phone call to Malone so she could come and get me.

Ten minutes later, I was with Carleen and in front of the magistrate. Carleen stood behind me. The foyer behind had officers walking to and from and the vending machine had two

91

male officers standing next to it drinking coffee and nattering over an arrest they'd both made earlier.

The magistrate looked up at me: another woman. Her face looked like a box, square jaw, manly features. Her hair had a clip in the back making it an upsweep that pinched her entire face into looking like a Klingon. "What happened tonight?" she asked in a husky voice.

"I failed the Olympic trials for field events," I said with a bit of disdain and humor.

Neither one of them thought it was funny.

With pursed lips, the magistrate asked, "What's your occupation?"

"I work for the state as a control monitor." I said this as she looked over the papers. I hoped it would work. The truth as euphemism.

"Carleen, take her down to the women's section," she said.

"Can I make a call? I'd like to get out tonight if possible," I said nicely.

"Oh, no, you're spending the night with us. DUI's always do. Go ahead, Carleen, take our gymnast down to the women's section and get her into a cell."

Thank God the occupation question was over. I hoped that no one would get wind of this since I was in a different county. The smartest thing I could have done—get arrested in a different place. Stupid but smart. I was sensing my own theme.

Carleen took me to the women's section of the jail and went into a small room where I had to take all of my clothes off in front of her, bend over, spread my cheeks and cough. I was given inmate's clothing, an inmate's handbook, and some toiletries. Then I was escorted down the hall. No rights. I had no rights.

Finally, there was a phone on the wall. "Can I make my call now?"

"Yep. You just got a few minutes. So, hustle up."

Thank God Malone had kept her same home phone number for years, otherwise I wouldn't have remembered anyone's number as they were all programmed in my cell.

I dialed furiously and nervously.

Her phone rang. Come on, Malone. Be there. Be there for me. I looked up at the clock on the wall: nine thirty p.m. I had been in-processing for over two hours. On the fifth ring, she answered.

And then the phone from where I was calling said, "Collect call from Greene County jail will you accept the charges?" A slight pause and then I heard a voice on the other end say, "Hey, Malone, this sounds funny…it's a collect call from Greene County jail."

It was Sammie's voice. Sammie had picked up the phone. Jesus H. Christ. Pagan. Pagan. Pagan. "Sammie!" I yelled. "It's me! It's Carrie. Don't hang up!"

"Carrie?" Sammie asked. "Yes, I'll accept the charges."

"Sammie. I'm in jail. Can you guys come and bail me out?"

"Sure, hang on. Let me get Malone." I could hear her walk away. My own microphone. Cichetti would be proud.

There was some rustling of the phone. Then like a sweet melody, a voice of comfort. "Hey, you okay?" It was Malone's first question. My best friend. My new attraction.

"What's Sammie doing there?" I asked.

"Are you okay?"

"What's she doing there, Malone?"

"Nothing, we're finishing a movie."

"What movie?"

"Jesus, Carrie, we're just watching a movie and you're calling from jail. I think your storyline has more importance here. What happened?"

"DUI."

"What did you blow?"

"I should have blown the cop?"

"Carrie, shut up. What did you blow?"

"Point one O," I said. "I'm screwed, Malone, absolutely screwed. I'm going to lose my license."

"I don't think that's the true issue here, Carrie. Do you need us to come and get you?"

"I have to stay the night. Can you get me first thing in the morning?"

"Yeah. I'm calling subfinder for the both of us to get the first half of our day covered."

"Good idea. Malone?"

"What?"

"Have you kissed her?"

"Who?"

"Sammie. Have you kissed her?"

"Carrie, shut up. You've got other things to worry about. We need to talk."

"Why can't you tell me. You have, haven't you!"

Carleen came over and tapped on her wrist. Time's up!

I covered the phone and asked Carleen. "About what time do you think I'll get out of here?"

"When the sun comes up, we let out all the criminals," she said and smiled wide. "Now, you need to get off the phone."

"As early as you can, Malone. Thank you. And, whatever you do, don't kiss Sammie..."

"I'll be there. Don't worry. You'll be okay."

When we hung up, my heart sank to the floor. I wanted to flop down on it.

Carleen escorted me to the cell and put me in with two others: a white girl was asleep on the bottom bunk; a black girl on the top bunk was staring at the ceiling. I was relegated to the floor with my handbook and toiletries. Carleen closed the door with a thud and locked it.

Sitting down, I leaned into the corner of the cell and raised my knees up to my chest and hugged them to me. My head hurt and I was thirsty. Glancing at the metallic toilet two feet from me, I suddenly thought of Melissa Fortunata locked in her temporary cell just a few days earlier. My paradigm was in alignment with hers but I would not shift, could not shift, did not want to shift. How was I like Melissa Fortunata? An educably mentally retarded girl who could say about ten words? How was I like her? Then I thought of Elizabeth Cichetti asking her to marry her over the loudspeaker. I laughed out loud, then I went into a downward spiral. I thought of Sammie kissing Malone. Keep your mitts off her, I thought. Then it was the enow's of my fifth-period class. I thought of Snodgrass and the GSA kids fighting Tulio and Jack.

Criminal. I was a criminal. I did not sleep thinking about Maya Angelou's *I Know Why the Caged Bird Sings*. And, then about how retarded I was. And, then I thought for the first time in a long time that I was wrong. I'd been using that word, retarded, wrongly.

I was a teacher and I was wrong.

Then, I leaned back in the corner, put on my imaginary dunce cap and fell asleep.

Hours later, the smell of my own beer breath and impending thirst awakened me to the morning light that came through the cell's window. Standing up, I stretched and pulled up my baggy jailhouse pants and walked the eighteen inches to the windowsill. On it were scratchings from other inmates. There was a scraggily engraving of *I heart John Dithers;* another engraving of *I was Here 12/10/06;* another engraving that said *FUCK this Place;* and then there was a series of etched arrows that trailed up the gray painted wall, and then as far as the engraver could etch, the last arrow pointing toward the outside but blocked by the concrete slab. With my finger, I traced the arrows to where they led toward the window and pressed my face against the concrete slats that let in the light. I could see the sky.

For the first time, I knew the stupidity of my drinking and the well of loneliness in my heart came up from a pressure I did not know or feel or comprehend. I placed my hand in between my breasts to hold the welling back but it was too late as the tears drew down in tiny pools, tiny rivulets to settle in the corners of my eyes. One tear came down when the woman on the lower bunk wrestled with her covers and began to awaken. I turned and wiped the tear and then with my index finger I retraced the arrows once more, then moved away from the window.

"Damn, it's hot in here," came the woman's voice from the

lower bunk. "Feels like I died and went to hell. Is this hell?" She gazed up at me.

"Close to it, I think," I said, and then slid back down into the corner I'd occupied all night. The cell held three people but wasn't fit for one. The cinder block room felt raw with its own funkiness. The old walls were gray and the floor was harder than slate and gritty from shoe dirt and dust.

The woman struggled with getting the covers completely off of her in such disgust that she hurled them to the floor and then she sat straight up in the bunk. "I need to ask Carleen, aka Robo-Cop, if she can open the door and turn a fan on or something."

Laughter came from the top bunk. "Robo-Cop. Janeen, you sure are funny. And if you think she's goin' to open that door, you're trippin'."

Janeen looked at me. "Can you ask her to open the door?"

"Me?" I pointed to myself.

"Yeah, you. You're the closest to the door aren't you? Ask her. Come on!"

I got up and peered through the square-shaped barred glass. Carleen was sitting on a chair outside the cell near where the phone was hanging on the wall. She was flipping through a magazine and a small fan was pointing at her. For some reason, the heat in the jail was up too high—everyone was hot.

Knocking on the window, I hoped to get her attention because I was slightly scared of the two female inmates who were now rising before me. What were they in here for? Drugs? Prostitution? Armed robbery? Murder?

On the fifth bang at the window, Carleen looked up and said, "What?" and shifted in her seat like it was the biggest inconvenience to speak and move at the same time. Oh, the energy.

I yelled. "Can you open the door and point the fan in here? Janeen is hot," I said it with such conviction. Then, like a balloon had suddenly popped, Janeen and the top-bunk girl started to laugh.

"You hear that, Tasha? Our roomie's gonna get Carleen off

her ass and open the door."

"Yeah," Tasha said. "Like you think she's gonna burn the extra calories to get off her white ass to open a jail cell for us. Robo-Cop!"

"What's your name?" Janeen scratched her head and looked at me intently.

"Carrie," I said demurely.

"Carrie, you're stupid. That Robo-Cop ain't gonna open that door."

"Then why'd you ask me to do it?" I asked.

From the top bunk, Tasha turned over and said, "Because you the newbie in this house girl. We gotta get you to try all sorts of things." She paused. "Yeah, Tasha, she retarded, brain been reduced in size or something. Why don't you ask Carleen if she'll bring us some smack. Go ahead we know you can do it. Walnut brain. Crystal meth, maybe?"

"You got it right Janeen, must be her first time in the hole."

Janeen looked at me. "What's you in for?"

I didn't look at either one of them. "DUI," I said.

Tasha laughed. "Janeen, you know what DUI means?"

"No, Tash. What?"

"Dumb and Under the Influence."

"That's the acronym I get with being with you two."

At first they didn't get it and then Janeen looked at me with fiery eyes, "What did you just say to us? You using big words with us? You think we don't know what you just said to us?"

Tasha hung her legs over the bunk and looked at me with the same intensity. "What's wrong with you, you dumb bitch!" And, down she came, practically banging Janeen's head on the way. She stood there and then leaned against the beds.

Keenly aware that my big mouth had gotten me into a potential jailhouse brawl, I tried to apologize. Just then, a key entered the door's tumbler, and Janeen spit on the ground.

Unlocking the door, Carleen stepped back and said, "Carrie Tomlinson, your people are here to pick you up. Let's go."

Divine intervention.

# Chapter 10

At seven a.m., I was released from institutionalized Greene County jail. I was like Alice in Wonderland as I walked through the initial processing area. I could see Sammie, Charlotte and Malone: but everything was small and weird. By the way they were standing and shifting their feet, I could tell they were worried. All three had their arms crossed. Sammie was standing next to Malone. I squinted to see the distance between them. Charlotte had on her red running outfit. Speculating, I'm sure, that we'd get me back to my house and she could run on the trails beside the farm next to me.

The walk through the looking glass was a long one, and I rotated my fingers around the ring I had received back from my jailers. Carleen was out of sight and Janeen and Tasha were still in the cell with the etched engravings that would be there till they tore the jailhouse down. My dully beating heart felt tired and my energy was low but it was sure good to lay my eyes on what seemed like Charlie's dyke-angels standing before me.

"Hey, you okay?" Malone asked, and then put her arms around me.

Sammie sidled beside me. "You look like shit. Any cute girls in there?" She popped me on the shoulder.

"Two really cute ones," I responded, releasing Malone and darting a look into her eyes before quickly reaching for Charlotte.

Charlotte hugged me and said, "What did you blow?"

"Point one O," I said. "It's good to see you."

Sammie slapped me on the back. "Well, how did you spend your first visit to jail?"

"Hopeful that it is my last." I slapped her on the back. "Let's go!"

Outside the jail, we all piled into Malone's rainbow-stickered Subaru to travel the forty miles back to Charlottesville. Bed. I just wanted a bed. And, then I did what I thought I wouldn't do. The burn in my eyes welled up and tears pooled in the corners so I thought they might spatter the window if I blinked too hard.

I was up front with Malone and Sammie and Charlotte drilled me with questions. Malone rolled through the parking lot around police cars and front-end loaders and deputy sheriffs coming in to relieve the night shift. Two oversized female deputy sheriffs chatted beside a tree near the complex of buildings and two inmates in martensite chains were being escorted by another deputy through the front doors we just came from.

Charlotte put her hand on my shoulder. "Well, Carrie, we'll get you home and you can get something to eat and then if you want, you can go for a run with me. Sweat out some of the jailhouse rock." She muffed my hair.

"Why don't you meet me at Ray's later after I do my run to Richmond, I'll be your DD and you can tell me all about it." Sammie hit my shoulder and a tear fell from my right eye. I wiped it with my shirt.

"How's Fortunata been since the incident?" I asked Malone,

99

ignoring Sammie and her request.

"Fine. I think she's fine." We passed two truck stops on Route 29 and Malone shifted lanes.

"What do you think those boys did to her?" I asked. "I mean, do we know what they did to her before they locked her in?" The pastoral scenery of 7-Elevens and dive bars mixed in with the mountains gave the landscape I stared at a kind of ironic schizophrenia.

"We may never know. Cichetti told me that there was some yelling, but she couldn't give me any specifics. Why are you interested?"

"Come on, Malone. You know I care about those girls…"

Mistake.

The car suddenly swerved and bounced over into the right emergency lane and Malone threw the car into park. "Carrie Tomlinson!" she yelled.

Uh-oh. I looked back at Charlotte and Sammie. Sammie's hand was on Charlotte's knee in a rigid grip and their eyes were bugged out at Malone.

"You don't care about anyone but yourself. Do you hear me?" Malone jumped out of the car. I wiped the tears off my tired face and my jaw dropped as she scooted around the car like a midget on crack.

"Roll your window down!" She banged on my window.

"What should I do?" I asked Charlotte and Sammie.

"Down!" They said in melodic unison.

Rolling down the window was another mistake. Malone half leaned in and barked at me in such an insinuating tone I wasn't sure if I should laugh, cry, or kiss her all at once.

"First of all," she said with her index finger jutting out.

"Careful," Sammie said, "it may be loaded."

"First of all," Malone started again. "Don't say a thing, Charlotte," she warned as she cut her eyes to her. I turned around and saw her throw her hands up in the air then shrug.

"Is this an intervention?" I asked.

"Shut your mouth, Carrie and let me talk." A tiny bit of spittle came out on her lower lip. "You're not helping anyone, Carrie. You're not helping me with the GSA. I've asked you sixteen times to help me organize my writing for Lobby Day at the General Assembly. You're not helping with Elizabeth Cichetti. You just let her run all over the place and you don't keep tabs on her. It's all amuck. Then the only thing you care about besides yourself is your basketball team, but that's not going well because you're practically hungover every day at school and you can't focus on the needs of your students. Then, I heard from your next-door neighbor at school that you didn't even lift a finger to help the fight. Not one finger. And what do you do. The only thing you do. Send Elizabeth Cichetti and Melissa Fortunata back to my room. And, now you've gotten a D damn U damn I. You could get fired, for Christ's sake, Carrie."

"It happened in Greene County…not Albemarle," I threw out impishly.

"That's going to be to her benefit, don't you think, Malone?" Charlotte asked from the back of the car. Advocate. Good girl, Charlotte.

"Malone," I asked. "Is this the part where I kiss you?" I laughed through more tears.

"Oh, God, you are incorrigible, Carrie Tomlinson. And, hopeless. Let's go."

"Sammie, do you think I'm incorrigible?" I asked.

Sammie put her hand on my shoulder again. "Yes, and meet me at Ray's tonight like, okay? I want to talk to you." She said this as Malone came huffy-puffy around the front of the car and then flopped in the driver's side. She scooted her seat closer to the dashboard so that she was driving with both hands clenched on the wheel like she was on the ride of her life. White-knuckled and brash and trying to save those special kids, regardless of IQ or sexuality: Audra Malone. I'd been trying to tell her for years that no one could be saved and she never listened.

This was a good thing.

Even though she was boiling berserk mad, Malone was a slow driver and it took us an extra twenty minutes to get to my house.

Everyone came in and Malone marched directly to my kitchen to wash the overflowing dishes in the sink.

I came up from behind her and put my hand on her shoulder. She did not turn around from washing a glass cup.

"Audra Malone," I said. "I know I drink a lot. I know I cruise women a lot. I know I make mistakes…"

"The mistakes are getting bigger, Carrie," she said, and then placed the washed cup in the drainer. "You need to…" And then she trailed off.

"What?" I asked.

"You need to get some help. Ever since Susan died, you have gone downhill. It's like you're standing still waiting for her to come back. Carrie, she's not coming back and your behavior is worse and worse and worse. It's like you don't even care."

"Audra, I do care. Where's my support here? I'm the one who was locked up last night."

"And, I think that's a good thing," she said as she grabbed another dish.

And then I grabbed her arm and turned her around.

"How is it a good thing that I was in jail last night? That's a rotten thing to say. I'm a good teacher and a good coach. Well, damn it…I was a good teacher and coach. I don't know. Maybe I still am. I don't care what you say. That stuff in here." I tapped on my chest. "That stuff never goes away. Susan is in here, too. Sometimes, she's the only thing I can hold onto."

"But, you have to move past her. Are you going to keep holding onto my arm?"

"Malone, I need to tell you something." I let go of her arm.

"What? What do you need to tell me?" Her huffiness exhaled half of her right lung.

I stepped back and peeked into the living room. Sammie and Charlotte were conversing on the leather sofa near the bay window. Sammie was "like this" and "like that" and Charlotte looked at me and winked. *Stay here,* I mouthed.

"Come out on the deck, Malone."

"Okay," she said. "Why can't you tell me in here? Your kitchen is a mess. I want to walk River…maybe we can take her for a walk and talk?"

Ignoring her, I opened the French doors to my small deck from which a stone pathway led to the ancient swing hanging off the ancient oak. Malone threw down a dirty kitchen towel and gave in and stepped out on the deck, which opened wider into a green vista that gave way to the three mountainous ridges that layered each other in curvy yet geometric succession. I suddenly felt as if I were riding a light wave. My belly was empty but the view and the air filled me for the moment.

Malone sat on the rust-colored Adirondack chair and I sat in the one next to it.

"I'm sorry if I hurt your feelings, Carrie. You are a bandersnatch of a woman; a true rapscallion. I don't know how your parents ever contained you."

"Malone, please don't talk about my snatch. And what's a bander?"

"Shut up," she said back. "Is that all you ever think about?"

"When's the last time you…you know? Did you kiss Sammie?" I asked, looking away.

"No. And the last time wasn't as long ago as you think," she said, drinking from her glass of water.

"Nineteen ninety-nine?" I asked.

"Shut up."

"It was. It was nineteen ninety-nine with that Reba girl from the carnival?"

"Yes."

"Malone?"

"What?"

"That was ten years ago."

"Do you want a prize for your math abilities?"

"It sucks to be in jail," I said after a moment.

"You suck all the time." And she smacked me on the thigh.

I grabbed her hand. "Malone?"

"Yes, are you going to let go of my hand?"

"No, letting go is something I don't do. You know. Beer.

103

Susan. Women."

"We need to help Elizabeth and Melissa, Carrie. It's important. A school board member has contacted Snodgrass and they want a hearing to talk about what has come down. It's bigger than you think."

"Will you listen to me for a second?" I let go of her hand. "I don't know how to say this, but I had some time in jail last night and it's been going on in my head for a little bit, you see. Strange..." I hesitated.

Malone just regarded me and turned back to the vista and the red-headed woodpecker now knocking into my oak tree.

For an eternity, we sat in silence. In my mind's eye, I thought back to the series of events that had unfolded in the last few days: the declaration of marriage, my loss of Elizabeth Cichetti, my incomprehension that Melissa Fortunata could be dragged by a bunch of bullies into a dank, dark bathroom for them to do what boys do—swear, piss on her, and perhaps touch her—I had to stop that thought. Defile. Why would anyone want to defile a girl who was mute?

Malone crossed her legs. "Well, what is it, Carrie. Whatever it is I hope you'll help me with this GSA problem I've inherited. I need assistance and if you can get out of your ego for a while, I think you might be some help."

Sammie came out the door. "Hey, I have to go to work. I'm already running late and I need to get the produce to Richmond today. Charlotte's going to ride with me, like, because she's got nothing better to do and wants to check out that weird train wreck of a tunnel I was telling you guys about."

"I wouldn't mind seeing that, too, someday," Malone said. "See you. Have fun."

"Carrie?" Sammie addressed me. I turned to Sammie. "See you, like, tonight at Ray's?" she asked.

"Yeah, like maybe like." It was hard not to mock Sammie for fun. She kicked my chair from behind.

"Hey, be careful. You can't kick an ex-con when they're down. At any rate, we've got to get to school in a little while. I feel hungover and tired and hungry. But, if the winds of change can help me with Malone, I'll be there."

"Whatever…" Sammie closed the doors and a few minutes later I could hear both Charlotte and Sammie nattering at each other as they got in Charlotte's car to leave to get the lettuce and fruit truck to drive to Richmond.

"Perhaps when the general assembly is in session, we can go see that train wreck?" Malone asked.

"I'm the train wreck, Malone. Haven't you gotten the memo? When are you going to the general assembly, anyway?" I asked, and put my feet up on the wooden ottoman.

A breeze came swift and sudden from the west. I shivered and rubbed my wrists where they had been cuffed the night before. Looking to the west for a second, I turned and faced Malone squarely to listen.

"In early February for lobby day. I'm helping Equality Virginia with some issues and resolutions that need helping."

I asked, "Will that hurt your job?"

"Nah. I don't think so. Just something I'm interested in. You should come with me. I need a sidekick, you know." She smacked me on the thigh and I thought this was my in. Should I pray on this one? Oh, God! Here I go…

"Malone. Here it is," I said, like I was laying cards out on a poker table. "I know we've been friends for many years and you've helped me through Susan's death and all that…but I have to tell you. You're going to think I have three heads. I—lately—have had this attraction for you. Okay, so don't look at me funny. It just happened recently and I…"

"You're kidding," she said again, smacking me on the thigh. She looked as if the words went right through her as she stoically stared at the ancient swing.

"Yes, and quit smacking me on the thigh. I'm damaged goods."

"You're kidding and, yes, you are damaged goods," she said. Her eyes were squinty and two robins quickly darted from the underbrush.

105

"No, I'm not kidding Malone. Don't be dense. I know it sounds weird but it's true."

"You're attracted to me—Audra Malone?" Malone said this and put her hands to her heart. She made a funny furtive glance and then nothing.

"Duh, yes, that's what I've been trying to CUH-MUNE-I-CATE to you!" I said back.

"Carrie. Don't be stupid," she said.

The wind flared up again, stronger this time. Malone's bangs went down into her blue eyes.

"Okay, if one more person calls me stupid or dumb or retarded—" I stood.

"You're not retarded. That would be a compliment. Just stupid. We've been friends for fifteen years. Good friends. Best friends. I've watched you through it all. The death of Susan—the love of your life—the drinking, the spiral downward of almost losing your house because you mortgaged it to the hilt then couldn't afford it. I've washed eight million coffee cups and have listened to your late-night phone calls blubbering about this girl and that girl. You're a mess, Carrie." She flung her hands in the air.

"But, Malone, listen to me—" I gestured in the air both arms and hands up as high as I could get them. My mockery.

Malone stood up and paced about, talking with her hands and counting things as she enumerated them. "That's just it, Carrie, I've been listening to you for fifteen years. When do you listen to me? I've asked you to help me with all kinds of things. Carrie, can you help me put my lawn mower in your Jeep so I can take it to Lowe's? Carrie, can you help me with the decking I want to put on the back of my house like yours so I can have a deck, too? Carrie, can you take care of River when I go to the Charlottesville Home? I had to make her a therapy dog because I couldn't count on you. Now I can take her with me. Carrie, can you help me paint the kitchen? Carrie, can you find me at least one of your friends to date? And, then you send me Sammie the fruit truck driver who is adorable but she's like, like, like so not my type?"

"You think she's adorable?" I asked.

"See there you go. You never listen and you ask the wrong questions. Did you hear me about the school board and the hearing about Elizabeth Cichetti and Melissa Fortunata?" She sat down and grabbed a magazine in passive-aggressive disdain.

"Yes," I said after a moment, impishly.

The magazine smacked to the floor. "Did you hear me when I asked you about all those other things and then there are probably fifty more and now you're telling me you have this attraction for me. Don't you think you're being just a little mental? You just got out of jail! I'm your buddy, not your soon-to-be lover. And, why would you think that just because I'm a plain-jane-on-the-short-side frumpy special ed. teacher that I might be interested in you? You exemplify everything I wouldn't want in a partner except that you're attractive and funny."

"So, those two count: attractive and funny? I can be the other things, Malone…"

"I'm leaving. I need to get to school and so do you."

"Malone…wait. Do you want a puppy?"

"Jesus, where did that come from? You know River is the only dog I want. You should come with us when we go to the Charlottesville Home. We go on our fourth visit next week. Besides, I can't afford a puppy."

"I just thought…I don't know what I'm thinking, Malone. I said it, so there. I found that I'm attracted to you—okay. Maybe it is weird but that's just how I feel."

Malone crossed her legs and arms, her thick hair waved in the wind. "Well, I think you're tired and not thinking right. Why don't you go take a shower? I'll go home and come back and get you and we'll go to school together. Okay, I appreciate your confession, but right now, I need to get my best friend to work."

"Malone?"

"Yes."

"Have you ever thought about me that way?"

"Once, but it faded. That's the truth, Carrie."

"When?"

"When Susan cheated on you...slept with your other best friend you don't have anymore...Amy...remember? And you nearly lost your marbles. You were at my house for almost two weeks straight. Remember that?"

"Yes."

"Go get in the shower, Carrie."

"Why do you think I stayed with Susan after that, Malone?"

"I think she was the one who stayed with you, goofy. Now go get in the shower. I'll be back in an hour to get you."

"Malone?"

"Yeah."

"Thank you."

"Oh, for Christ's sake, don't start thanking me now. If you do, it'll cost you...see you in a bit."

"Malone, what's the Charlottesville Home?"

"Google it."

Malone went through my French doors and then marched out through the front door. I watched her the entire way as she stuck her hand in her pocket for her keys. I watched the slowness of her gait, her pear-shaped body ambling to her Subaru. Once in, I saw her scoot her seat clear to the dashboard. I smiled at this.

I'd hoped she would turn around and catch my gaze as she put her car into gear.

She did not.

# Chapter 11

Lynchburg High School was the visiting team we were to play the night I got out of jail. My girls took the floor at seven thirty p.m. after our Junior Varsity team lost to Staunton's JV squad sixty-three to thirteen.

The old gym stank of sweat and sneakers and the wooden bleachers were chipped and sticky and holding a small number of staunch fans from both sides. The Mountain Dog had his blue uniform on and was lying on the floor next to the three cheerleaders who showed up because they were told to. Our season started three weeks earlier than the boys so that gym time and travel time were available.

Vickie, my small forward, and Pickle, my dribble-master point guard were the captains of the team and were huddled in the middle with the referees and the opposing team's captains when I lost sight of Cichetti. Earlier, I had spotted Fortunata at

109

the end of the stands, but as I scanned the small crowd, I couldn't see her either.

Spotting Eddie and Annie Cichetti, I felt a twinge of relief. Backup if I needed them. The rest of my players shot underneath our basket and Juanita Jones and Sheila Selden were helping one another pull off their warm-up pants. For a split second, I wondered about their sexuality then dismissed it. I thought about Malone and then felt a twinge in my stomach and dismissed that, too. But, just as I dismissed it, it came back in. The same repetition I'd had with her since the attraction began. In my head every day, every minute—enow!

I got up from the bench and decided I should take a quick check in the girls' locker room to see if the lovebirds had made it in there. My clipboard anchored to my side, my game face on, I slid over to the door and unlocked it to see if my theory was correct.

"Cichetti! Cichetti!" I peeked around the lockers. Nothing. "Fortunata! Fortunata! Are you guys in here? Hello?" Checking around all lines of lockers. Nothing. Hmm. Where were they? Perhaps they hadn't got locked in as I'd suspected. Jetting back outside to the gymnasium, I saw Snodgrass coming my way. He put his hand up, stopped and then waved me over.

"Hey," I said as I approached. My brown loafers clacked on the floor, and I pulled up my loose khakis.

"We've got a small problem. Minor. Maybe you can help. Or I can get Eddie Cichetti to come." Snodgrass pulled at the length of his faded blue tie as he said this.

"What is it?" I asked.

"Elizabeth is sitting at the scorer's table and won't budge. Look."

At the scorer's table, Elizabeth sat next to Fortunata. She was right behind the microphone and the gentleman who normally announced the games was leaning into her ear saying something. Fortunata had her frog wound up and jumping backwards on the table.

"Oh, Christ! Behind a microphone again," I moaned.

110

"My sentiments exactly. This has to stop, Carrie. And this GSA thing has gotten out of control. We have a hearing next week and now one of the GSA parents has been calling me and asking why we can't have same-sex dancing at the November dance. You know how that works. Carrie, can you get Elizabeth away from there without causing a scene? Suddenly, half the school is behind these two and the other half isn't. It's starting to go viral. Pretty soon, the whole community will be up in arms."

Locking in on Cichetti, I mumbled something to him that I would take care of it. Cichetti sometimes listened to me and sometimes did not.

When I approached the scorer's table, the announcer looked at me, pointed at them and then shrugged. He moved back. Out of the corner of my eye, I saw a few kids from my fifth period Enowers—one was Sherry Proffitt, who for the second day in a row had not had her poetry recitation ready. Nodding her way, I kneeled down next to Elizabeth, who wouldn't look at me.

"Hey, Cichetti girl. What's going on?" I turned to Fortunata and put my hand on her back. She squinched her shoulders back and resumed her frog flipping.

"I'm going to announce the game, Mith Tomlinthon!" Cichetti said, hands up in the air. "I'm going to announce the game. Fort is going to help."

"Elizabeth Cichetti, you're going to have to come sit with me on the bench. If you want, Fort can sit with us."

"No."

"Yes."

"No." Then she twiddled her orange bracelet.

Silence.

"Elizabeth Cichetti?" I asked.

"Yeth. It'll be okay. I know how. I know how to talk. Fort doesn't but I do." She patted Fort on the back and then resumed her stare at the microphone.

"I'm going to have to get your dad, Cichetti girl."

Silence.

More silence. The referee came over and asked if there was a problem. I explained it away by pointing at the two at the table.

One of my players, Robin Altoona, trotted over and asked if she could help.

"Will you go get Mr. Cichetti?"

And then, a few girls behind me began to chant: "Cichetti…Fortunata…Cichetti…Fortunata…" The banter started and then about twenty people began to chime in as well.

I turned around. "Stop! Stop egging them on!"

"Come on Ms. Tomlinson. Let Elizabeth do the announcements!" It was one of the GSA kids, Brandon Smart, who'd been out of school the day the brawl started. He was a senior wrestler and straight. "They love each other. Let her do it, Ms. T. Come on…"

Robin Altoona showed up with Eddie Cichetti and in a nanosecond, Cichetti left her post and took Fortunata with her. They sat down at the end of the bench and Eddie's lips tightened as he leaned over and spoke to both of them.

The incident ended. The game started fifteen minutes late. A technical foul was given to our team and the Staunton girls began with two extra points and the ball. It pissed me off but I was too tired to deal with it. Too tired with any of it. I wanted it to be over so I could go to Ray's and have that beer with Sammie.

Once the ball went to our side, our offense took on what looked like a chess game. No one moved. Janet and Cody who did well in the two and three spots respectively decided that passing the ball and moving in to the open spot, basketball fundamentals, was a concept so foreign that it was like they'd taken up a completely different sport of standing and freezing.

"Move to the open spot!" I yelled to Janet. "Jenny and Colleen—off the blocks and pick either side. Go. Go. Go. Robin's wide open. Skip pass. Skip pass. Look. Look. Look!"

The lead was completely in our feet. I couldn't even believe we could make it past half-court to play defense. Terri and Vicki both got in early foul trouble which meant Jenny and Colleen went in without enough practice time. Their fundamentals weren't as sound, therefore, once again, turnovers turned into points.

We lost forty-nine to fifty-eight. When I talked to my team in the locker room afterward, I told them that we needed to work on some fundamentals and that we'd had a few bad games to start the season but with some extra practicing, we could be in shape for the next game.

Pickle spoke up at the end of my very bad coach's talk and said, "Coach T., if Elizabeth hadn't have done what she done, then we'd been off to a better start."

"I know, Pickle, but those fourteen turnovers might have played a part, too, don't you think?"

This shut her up.

"Where is Cichetti?" I asked.

"Right here, Mith Tomlinthon! Right here." I hadn't seen her but she was at the back of the locker room. "Where's Fort?" I asked, pissed that she'd heard Pickle say what she had said.

"She's gone home to sleep," she said. "Can I announce the next game?"

I was too tired to fight. "We'll see. We'll see." With that, Cichetti smiled and threw her green frog in the air that she and Fort were now sharing. "Can I go shoot, Mith T.?"

"Yes, Cichetti, go ahead."

She scampered outside. The fog in my head became thick with lack of sleep over my jail time.

I went to Ray's anyway. Got drunk. Sammie dropped me at home.

I did not look at Susan's picture in the kitchen. I went straight to bed and did not call Malone, even though I wanted to.

The weekend came and I laid low in my house, trying to clean. Everything was a disheveled mess. I had laundry to do and I tried not to let my stomach drop to the floor every time I thought of being in jail, every time I thought of Malone. The jail incident played over and over in my head, a broken record. In my treks through my home, I replayed the events of the evening; the smell of the jail cell like farts and burps mixed in with old dead skin cells. The heat of it. The arrows on the windowsill. The etchings.

Bleary-eyed and fuzzy, I ambled to the store on Saturday afternoon, and on the way drove by Malone's house. Her Subaru was in the yard but Sammie's produce truck was not. Sammie had told me at Ray's that she liked Malone, but perhaps she wasn't her type, like. It was the first time in the twenty-four hours since I became a criminal that I was relieved. Buying groceries and beer, I trekked by her house thirty minutes later and noticed timbers on the side of her house. Hmm. A deck? Wanting to pull in was overwhelmed by the need to just go home and bury myself in the bed with a twelve-pack of beer and some chips.

When I got home, I put everything away and began to wash the coffee mugs in my sink. Looking out my window at the cool October day, I watched my ancient swing do a languid sway in the Virginia breeze. I swallowed a quarter of the beer and returned to the dishes. The wind chimes on my deck bobbled and the greenery of my vista looked like a pasture of ocean touching the mountains which touched the sheltering sky. With a sudden fervency, my eyes became riveted to the stones on my windowsill and then more tranquilly to Susan's picture, nestled between the glass and the rock that said *grace*. In 1999, just four years before her death, Susan had come home from work at UVA Medical Center and told me she'd had an affair with Amy, a nurse where she worked. Once, just once, she had said to me, that it didn't mean anything and would I stay with her.

"You fucked up, Susan," I said aloud in my kitchen.

Pulling up a stool, I sat down with a whump and swallowed more beer. For several minutes, I stared at her picture and then I babbled some more. "Not sure what happened there with Amy. Okay, so I didn't want to have sex with you for almost a year. Was that it? Was it the fact that I had my own issues and you just went outside the relationship for a little love? The drinking issues? I was too drunk to have sex with you? Come on, honey? Tell me. Now all I'm looking for is a little love too, but as Audra tells me, I can only have it with young, attractive college students. Jesus.

114

Guess I'm getting back at you for what you did to me. How does that feel? God, was I always the hollow, shallow woman. Was I shallow with you? Maybe so. I am one shallow dumb bitch."

Swallowing the last of the beer, I opened another, sat down and continued my sloppiloquy. "I know you were mortified. I was too. Now look at where the fuck you are: dead. Not here. Left me for the cleanup? You've been dead four years, Susan. Well, I guess you know that on some level."

I screamed and threw my arms in the air. "How could the love of my life cheat on me? How could you do that? How could you? How could you? I think I'm still a bit pissed about it. Shallow and all."

Lying down on the kitchen floor, looking for more rhetorical questions, I finished my beer and threw it at the trash can and missed. "Good job, Coach T. Can't even make your own shots. Can't even make your own score. Gotta go on and tell Malone that you're attracted to her. Then she's gotta tell you what's good about you and what sucks about you. And, now you're talking to a dead person and lying on your kitchen floor and NO ONE'S LISTENING TO YOU."

The wind chimes bounced a tubular melodic tone. "Shut up!" I barked at them. "You don't sound that great."

I stood up and opened the door to the fridge for another beer. By beer six, the poet in me had emerged and I decided to write. I did not want to write about the plums in the icebox as William Carlos Williams had done. I wanted to write about something else.

Legal pad in hand, I went into the living room and bounced down on the leather couch.

I wrote and wrote and wrote. Finishing the twelve-pack of beer in four hours on a Saturday afternoon. Charlotte called and asked if I needed anything. I told her more beer and a movie.

Later, in the early part of the evening, Charlotte came by with a bottle of wine, some cooking magazines, and a soft voice. She put a blanket over my legs, cleaned up the poetry collection I'd written and turned the TV on with the sound off. The smell of garlic and onions sautéing in the kitchen reached my nose for a nanosecond, then I fell asleep.

In the morning Charlotte was still there and when I awakened with my larger-than-life head, I asked her if she thought I was a bad person like Malone thought.

"Oh, honey. Malone, doesn't think you're a bad person. She just needs you sometimes like we all do. That's it, really. Sometimes people just need each other for the simplest things." She filed her nails and smiled at me.

"I love you, Charlotte."

"I love you, too, Carrie."

"Charlotte?" I asked, trying to pull my hung over body up. I felt shloggy.

"Yeah," she said, sipping her coffee and then opening a magazine.

"Do you think I have a drinking problem?"

"Honey," she said matter of factly, "we all think you have a drinking problem."

"Good." I lay back down. "I was just wondering."

"Carrie, wonder away. Wondering is good for you."

Spotting my poetic diatribe from the night before, I wondered for split second if Charlotte had read them. I looked quickly to her.

"Don't worry," she said. "I only read the first page of the one sitting on the coffee table. You're not bad, Carrie. Have you told the love of your life about this?"

"Who? Susan?" I asked.

"No, Malone. You can't fool me by calling her Audra Malone in the poem. I may be dense but that sure gave it away."

"Oh, God!" I put my hand over my mouth. "I can't believe the cat is out of the bag. Can we go to Green Top and kill ourselves today?"

"Not today. No suicide today. I'm in training for the marathon. Do you want to go for a run down at Campbell Park and then go get some coffee?" Charlotte stood up.

"Well, you don't seem very surprised," I said.

"Carrie, goofy, nothing has surprised me over these past few years. But more recently, we've got two special ed. kids stirring up a school and now a community. Did you see the sign down by Ray's? It says, *Elizabeth heart Fortunata—Go all the way SRHS*. That's more surprising than anything."

"What does that mean, go all the way?" I asked.

"There are people in the community who want them to get married. Legitimately. Or even if it's a civil union. It's given the community something to talk about. And, frankly we need something to talk about besides the price of gas, the economic crisis, UVA football and what the crops are going to do. It's kind of like they don't have what normal people have, so why not let them get married. What harm would it do? Everyone's talking about it on Facebook and Myspace and I hear it's gotten the attention of a reporter at the town newspaper who's blogged about it."

I stood up and the covers fell on the floor. "It would do a lot of harm. Those two girls don't know what it means to get married. How the hell can a community be stupid enough to egg them on? I can't believe this. There's a hearing on Tuesday with the school board. Malone wants me to go—"

Charlotte laughed. "Good, you can give her your poem that obviously professes your love for her, Carrie."

"I was drunk when I wrote that."

"Drunks always tell the truth," she stated and then leaned over to stretch.

"Then I must be the fortune teller of Truth," I laughed.

Charlotte cracked her neck on both sides. "Honey, all you need is a deck of Tarot cards and a purple cone hat with some half moons and stars."

"Maybe for Halloween...I gotta get out of here. Charlotte, don't tell anyone about my legal pad profession of love for Malone." I lurched over and fell from the sofa to the floor.

Charlotte cocked her head at me. "Carrie, don't be stupid. You know I'm a gossip. If we're going to tell the truth, we might as well speak up. You can't keep silent anymore, honey. It's not your style. Jesus, it's the twenty-first century. Silence is way out of style. Haven't you heard?"

"Easier said than done," I said, staring up at the ceiling.

"Come on. Let's go for that run. Do you need some pen and paper in case you want to write a little epistle to Malone? Hmm. Maybe put it under her windshield wiper on the way home?" Charlotte stood up and stretched her triceps and then leaned over to get her hamstrings.

"I'm starting not to care, you know."

"About what?" she asked, then jogged to the kitchen to retrieve a bottle of water.

I yelled, "I'm starting not to care about anything. I just want to run away. Can you run away at thirty-eight?"

"Let's just go to the park and run. And, Carrie…" She came back into the living room and over to me.

"What?"

"You've got a zit on the side of your mouth…" she pointed, "right here on the left side." She swallowed her water and leaned to me and nearly touched it with her index finger.

"Oh, brother, let me go take care of it. Zits: the most disgusting yet fascinating body inventions of all time."

"Can I watch?" Charlotte said from the living room as I shuffled into the bathroom.

"No. God, no!"

Charlotte mocked me, "God! Yes!"

So, there went the zit and we went for a jog in Campbell Park.

Suicide is painful.

I passed by Malone's house twice on Sunday. Both times, her car was gone. The second time, I turned around and went to Ray's looking for I don't know what. It was the four p.m. Tea Dance and I was just in time to spot Sammie and a few of her acquaintances. For three hours I danced and drank beer. There was some chick from Ruckersville there who knew Sammie from the same produce business. The beat of the music thumped in my chest and I goggled around at anything and everything, including the bartender.

"Sammie?" I asked her, finally sitting down next to her.

"Yeah!" she said, leaning close to me in the booth.

"You think that girl, you know, would want to go out with me?"

Sammie smacked me in the back of the head. "Jesus Christ, Carrie! I already talked to Charlotte. She texted me half the poem you wrote to Malone. Don't you think you better try Malone before you start to cheat on her already?"

"What?" I couldn't hear her over the music.

"Go get Malone, DUMB ASS!" Then she repeated what I hadn't heard.

Shit, I thought. Charlotte. I'm going to kill her and love her all at the same time. Before I'd even gotten off the couch this morning, she'd texted half of Charlottesville that I was writing love poems to Malone.

I went home pulled up a chair to Susan's photo at my kitchen windowsill.

"Susan, I'm not going to cheat on Malone if she'll have me. She might not. She sees that I don't care half the time and that's my big fucking problem I have to overcome. My own sluggish, voiceless, bullshit of a bullshit of a voiceless..." I trailed off.

Give voice to the voiceless. It resounded in my head once, twice, three times. Then I slowly formed the words: "Give voice to the voiceless." Then I went and got my legal pad and wrote it down.

Voice to the Voiceless.

Melissa Fortunata was mute.

Elizabeth Cichetti was not.

Holy fucking epiphany.

Then I cracked open a beer to celebrate.

# Chapter 12

When Tuesday finally arrived, I somehow managed to make it through the doldrums of the day without talking to Malone. Or, perhaps she was putting me on ignore. I didn't know but was beginning to feel as if my heart had been jump-started. Pressing my hand between my breasts, I checked to see if it was still there and still beating. Felt like it.

After an early practice and only losing Cichetti once to the small gym, I scooted to the evening school board hearing that was being held in the library of our school. There were three school board members from our district on hand and a number of parents and students, including Eddie and Annie Cichetti and Nate and Gwendolyn Fortunata. The library smelled like oil and dust and there were stacks of books lying like tired soldiers on three shelving carts near the check-out desk.

Both Cichetti and Fortunata had been with me after practice.

It had been six thirty and almost completely dark outside. I'd gotten them Cokes from the vending machine and some Nabs to crunch on during the proceedings. Both sets of parents had explicitly asked for their children to be here now. Why, I wasn't sure. But, I was the last faculty member to have them with her. I would be the bearer of the news that Fortunata had stayed by my side almost the entire practice; Cichetti had shot the ball, and every now and again they would go behind the bleachers and kiss. I ignored it and told the team to think about defense and nothing else.

Malone was at the front of the line of plastic colored chairs that had a carpeted runway down the middle. She appeared bright and confident; my stomach dropped. People for the GSA and supporters for the Cichetti proclamation of marriage were ironically on the right side of the seats. Then there were the ones against the whole thing on the left side. An even fifteen or so on both sides. A faint smell of cigarette smoke filled my nose as I wrangled with my own retard and my own mute.

Slowly and arthritic-like, Snodgrass got up to speak. His tweed jacket hung from his shoulders and he pushed his reading glasses up on his nose and took a deep breath.

"Good evening ladies and gentlemen. I'd like to welcome you to Sterling Road High School: home of the Blues. We are committed to supporting our students and faculty in their endeavors to facilitate the mission of this county: to uphold the principles set forth in the code of conduct..." He cleared his throat. "Tonight we have three school board members here: Bruce Jenkins—" He pointed to Bruce who nodded. "And Carolyn Raymond and John Stovall." They nodded. Carolyn smiled. "These three board members are going to discuss what transpired here last week and what measures we need to put in place to ensure it will not happen again. Specifically, we are discussing the incident where Melissa Fortunata was locked in the boys' bathroom, and then the ensuing fight that was intiated by members of the GSA on two members of the junior class: Jack Ignatio and Tulio Grayson. For the record, both members of the

GSA and Mr. Ignatio and Mr. Grayson were given out-of-school suspension for fighting. The other piece of business we need to discuss is same-sex dancing as Ms. Malone of the exceptional ed department has brought this up as items for both the November dance and the Valentine's Day dance committees having already been formed."

There was a slight pause as everyone re-crossed legs and shuffled papers. Snodass kept his composure and I pined for a moment looking at Audra Malone. What was I going to do now? What was I going to do in this situation now? The light in me, the good in me was battling with the dark, the selfish and the egotistical. I needed to stop reading Eckhart Tolle. This guy was getting me more confused than I already was. Craning my neck backward I looked to the fluorescent lights and cracked my neck then reached into my pocket to feel Flip the frog. I adjusted my watch then looked at the floor for an answer in the flat speckled carpet that smelled like dirt and leather and grass and mold.

Fortunata burped and tore into her cheese crackers. I muffed her hair and watched Cichetti pull her crackers out and line them up on her right thigh. She placed one on Fortunata's thigh and Fortunata giggled. Then Fortunata replaced it back on Cichetti's thigh in the same manner. They loved to mimic each other. Monkey see, monkey do. Then they began laying them on my thighs. I let them do it and ate two of them before Cichetti saw my criminal mind and rotated her eyes back to Fort's thigh. I reached into my pocket and gave Flip to Cichetti.

I saw Nate Fortunata with his oxygen tank and Gwendolyn, his wife, sitting toward the front. Eddie Cichetti and Annie sat right behind them. Annie smoothed her hair out from the back of her jacket and Gwendolyn had combs through each side of her head. Everyone had their respective heads cocked to one side to figure out what in the world Snodass was talking about. Malone sat in front of the Fortunatas… She peered back and saw me. I waved and she waved back and winked. My stomach dropped yet again.

"Well," Bruce Jenkins started the meeting. "It looks like we need to discuss the matter and then establish what is going on with this GSA and why a fight broke out and then I think the rules of why we don't allow same-sex dancing will become crystal clear. A dance is between a boy and a girl; like marriage. See. You see." He said this at the close of each statement. See. You see.

"I think, ladies and gentlemen, that we are advocating here for a certain unhealthy political perspective if this GSA continues in the manner in which it has," Carolyn Raymond said, her tight brown suit as boring as she was.

"You see," Bruce Jenkins dropped in, "we need to enforce the code of conduct to make sure that the rights of all students are respected."

John Stovall leaned back, looked at his nails, flipped open his cell phone and said, "I agree."

Tulio Grayson slipped out to the side of the gaggle of people before me and as I was watching him, Cichetti pulled on my shirt.

"Mith Tomlinthon. I have to go to the bathroom," she stated.

After last week's episode, I wasn't about to let her go by herself. "Hang on." I picked up my clipboard. "I'll go with you." We both stood up and she showed me her UVA bracelet for the thousandth time.

"It's for luck." She smiled at me like Wonder Woman.

"Luck is good," I said back to her. "Sometimes you need a little luck."

"Sometimes you need a lot," Cichetti spittled out, some cracker flying with it.

"Fort, stay here and play with Flip," Cichetti ordered handing the frog to her.

Fortunata smiled delicately, almost placidly, "Flip." It was all she said and then she patted his head. Fortunata remained in her seat, content with Flip and where she was.

"Hold my hand," I said to Cichetti.

"Where's your bracelet?" she asked.

"At home on my dresser…I'll put it on soon."

"Soon. Soon. Soon." She mocked me, that Cichetti.

"Funny, you're so funny." I patted her head.

I hurried Cichetti out the back double doors to the library and down the front hall to the main office and around the corner to the girls' restroom. At that point, it did not even occur to me where Tulio Grayson had gone. The only thing on my mind was Malone.

Entering the putrid smell of the newly cleaned bathroom, I told her to hustle while I doodled out some basketball plays on my clipboard. I leaned against the wall and peered out the window on the wall nearest the sinks. Just barely, I could make out the moon. Spoon River came to mind. Where was that book?

Then through the door, he came.

"You like takin' care of retards, Ms. Tomlinson?" Tulio said. He had slithered in through the door like a cockroach. "Make you feel special?" He licked his lips in a way that was sexual and grotesque.

"Tulio, get out! This is a girls' bathroom. You've got no business being in here. Leave!" I pressed my clipboard to my chest and crossed my arms. Quickly, I looked and saw Cichetti's feet under the stall up on their tippy toes.

He stepped closer and I did not say a word aloud to Cichetti. I could almost feel his breath. It smelled like bourbon. He took his index finger and pressed it against my shoulder. "You know how hard this feels..." He pressed it against my shoulder again. "A few more minutes and that fat mute retard would have felt it, too. If her girlfriend hadn't gotten away, she would have felt it, too. That's what dykes want, right, a nice hard finger up their pussy?"

"Tulio, get out. Get out right now before I scream and turn you in."

"Awww. Come on now, you know that bar, Ray's? That queer bar? You wouldn't want to yell too loud, my father's disowned brother helps run that place. We know all about you. Ain't no secret." His greasy hair and trimmed goatee came closer to me.

My silent rage came out at him. "Tulio, you're just as trapped

124

as we all are. Trapped in this bathroom. Trapped in your rage over something you don't even understand. You're trapped in cultural and religious thinking. And now you're trapped into thinking you can scare me and a special ed. student into doing what? Feeling your stupid index finger on my shoulder and then putting it between my legs or her legs or Fortunata's legs to make you feel what? More like a man? That's the pussy way out Tulio. You're using power over another individual to strengthen you up. Whoa! Big boy that you are! I can't believe you pissed all over her head and shirt."

"Shut up!" It was all he could manage. "Shut the fuck up!"

"E-e-e-N-O-W! You small man, get out of here before your index finger shrivels up into nothing. Because that's all that it is. Get out of this bathroom. Get out of here, you burgeoning pedophile. What? Did your dad do something funny to you when you were a kid? Did he stick his finger in places where boys don't like it or maybe you did? Huh? Get out of her life and go back to the slimy hollow you came from. After I'm done with you, you'll have to go to a different state to get into a high school. Go harass someone else in a different state."

I threw my clipboard on the ground and poked him in the shoulder. Where the rage in me came from, I did not know. But, here it was helping me. The anger was helping. Fight fire with fire.

"Go! Get!"

He backed up and walked out.

"Cichetti?" I called to her through the stall door.

"Mith Tomlinthon?"

"You ready?"

"Yeah. Mith Tomlinthon? I still want to marry Fort," she said, coming out of the stall smiling. "I don't like that boy. He's mean." She hiked her pants up and washed her hands and then rubbed them dry on her khakis.

"Yeah. He's mean. Let's get out of here."

"Mith Tomlinthon. Can we go see a UVA game together?"

"Sure. Sometime. I'm just afraid I'll lose you like I always do."

"You don't lose me. I'm right here." She smiled her wide smile, looking up to me. "I'm your manager and you're the coach. I love you."

"I love you, too, Elizabeth Cichetti. Now, we have to be quiet when we go back into the library."

Opening the doors, I saw Malone standing up talking to the board. She was shaking and out of breath. I scanned the crowd for Tulio Grayson and did not see him. Motioning for Snodgrass, I jerked my head for him to come over. He obeyed.

"Tulio Grayson just harassed me in the bathroom with Elizabeth Cichetti. Did he come back in here?"

"I never saw him. Was he in here?"

"Yes, yes. He was up there behind the first row or two with Jack Ignatio...who, of course, I don't see anymore either."

"Write a referral when you go back to the office after the meeting. I'll call him up in the a.m. if he shows up." Snodgrass stood up straight to hear what Malone was saying. Then he slowly walked away dismissing the rest of my story, his eyes firmly on her.

"...and another thing. These kids of the GSA formed this group and approached me to start it. They wanted the same rights as the other kids and a way to speak up at certain national events like National Coming Out Day and the Day of Silence. Moreover, they want the right to express their kinship and love for each other by dancing at the school dances. Bottom line, they have a commitment to educate the greater school community and beyond. We see that they have been supporting the Cichettis and Fortunatas by showing their support of Elizabeth since she professed her love just recently in a statement that she wanted to marry her sweetheart, Melissa Fortunata, who happens to be in her special ed. class." Audra Malone took a much needed breath. She was fire engine red.

As I heard her say this, Fortunata twiddled her hands in front of her and began rocking back and forth. Gently and sweetly, Cichetti put her hand on her thigh and then I saw Fortunata look at it, smile, mumble something, then reach out and grasp it.

Vivian Jones said, "Yeah!" really loudly. She stood up and whacked her hands together.

Claire Austin high-fived Vivian back and said, "Yeah, Ms. Malone!"

There was a pause while we waited for Vivian to re-seat herself.

Malone finished her speech and resettled back into her chair. Several people around her, including the Cichettis, patted her on the back. You could almost feel her sweat exude itself and permeate the room.

"Well, I've got something to say." Mr. Fortunata got up and leaned against the chair in front of him while readjusting his breathing tube. "My daughter is twenty-one years old and never have I heard her profess any love to this Elizabeth Cichetti and I don't think it's right that this school and this principal and this GSA sponsor do the things they are doing to my little Melissa. She only has about ten words in her vocabulary and I've never heard her say anything about loving another girl. What I think is happening is that this Elizabeth Cichetti is manipulating the hell out of all of us—"

"Whoa, wait just a minute!" Eddie Cichetti stood up. "My daughter is the sweetest, kindest youngster on earth. She doesn't even know what manipulation is…so how can she—"

Bruce Jenkins intervened. "Mr. Cichetti, Mr. Cichetti, let him speak."

Eddie sat down with a whump.

Mr. Fortunata went on. "It isn't right. My daughter has been through enough. I don't want her kind and gentle ways to be dragged through someone else's cause. It isn't hers and it isn't mine! Now, her mother has been very upset by this." He looked at Gwendolyn. "She feels the same way I do. Melissa is our only child and I'm pretty sick with this stuff…" He grabbed the tube and waved it. "I want all of this to stop so we can move on with our lives. It's hard. We have a little trailer and Melissa helps, but I'm scared about what will happen to her once I'm gone and

127

I don't want my final months dragged out into some kind of high school community circus fair for equal rights. Hell, I think Melissa's straight."

There he said it. Melissa the mute was straight.

Then Bruce Jenkins and Carolyn Raymond called the meeting to some order and said that they would get back with Malone and the dancing and the GSA and all of the things that were discussed. Right now, all three school board members wanted Sterling Road High School to squelch what had happened to Melissa Fortunata and the brawl that had ensued. They also wanted to take up a committee with other schools on how to deal with GSAs and the rights thereof.

People began to shift in their seats as the meeting went on. I looked at the clock noting that I was getting hungry, too. I asked Cichetti for a cracker. She obliged.

"This kind of delicate situation takes a long time," Bruce Jenkins said. "We need to put the kibosh on this whole entire debacle and get some normalcy back here at this school and this town. We've got bigger things to worry about in this economic crisis of ours than who can dance with whom and what gender is right or not."

Carolyn Raymond said, "I'm more worried about fuel for our school buses than this. There are more important issues and we need to make sure we prioritize what is most important here."

Each set of parents, the Cichettis and the Fortunatas, got up and trudged slowly to the back of the room where I was stationed with their twenty-one-year-old lovers.

"Come on Melissa," Nate said as he struggled to breathe, "let's go."

Then as Melissa Fortunata was being whisked away as best as Nate could whisk her, she turned around and said something that the whole crowd heard.

"Elizabeth!" She stuck her arms in the air like she was scoring a touchdown.

Then, quickly, Elizabeth got up and ran to hug her.

It seemed to expunge everything that was said; a collective

aww could be felt from around the room.

I looked at Malone; she looked at me.

This time my stomach didn't drop. I winked at her and she rolled her eyes.

# Chapter 13

Tulio Grayson was in colossal trouble. In diabolical rage, I scribbled out the incident report after I'd sailed on the wind to get to the main office after the school board meeting. It was getting late, but my desire to get him in trouble usurped my desire to get home and drink beer. I re-wrote our entire bathroom conversation and as I was doing so, Malone walked in to check her mailbox. The front office lights were dull and dim and she did not see me. From the side hall, moonlight filtered in through the windows and as I furiously scratched what had happened in the bathroom, I leaned on the counter in front of the mailroom where the slots for referrals and detentions and school-related leave were in small cubbies. Feeling her movements, I decided to say something before I scared her.

"Malone," I whispered.

"Jesus Christ!" Malone turned around to face me in the

dark.

"No, me, Carrie," I said.

"Yeah, Jesus Christ would have been a little much after tonight's hearing. Just you is fine with me."

"Thanks for the accolade," I said, and my stomach dropped again. "I'm writing up a referral on Tulio Grayson. Did you see him earlier?"

"Yeah. He was sitting up toward the front with some hip-hop kids, I thought." Malone tossed some mail into the trash can, missed one, and then leaned over to pick it up.

"We had a disaster in the bathroom, but Snodgrass said he didn't see him."

Malone's face had returned to a normal bright red but I kept my mouth shut about it.

"Jesus," she said. "He was sitting two seats over from him during the first part of the meeting. How could you miss him? Tulio sticks out like a sore fat toe."

"Hmm. That's weird," I said.

"Yeah, it is. How do you think it went?" Malone leaned against the secretary's desk, crossed her arms and gazed right at me.

"You did really well. Want to go get a beer?"

She laughed. "Want to go get some tea?"

"Okay, you win this round. But, you are buying. Have you thought any more about my modest proposal from last week?" I asked.

"Yes. You know it was quite the proposal. How long did it take you to think of it?"

I leaned against the counter next to her. "A lifetime or so. Few things and people got in the way. Including me."

"Why the change of heart?"

"Are you looking for something poetic?" I asked.

She stood up straight and stretched her arms. I wanted to reach out and hug her but did not.

"I'm looking for some Earl Grey and some cream and a tea cookie." She smiled.

"I can only summon George Gray right now. Will he do?"

"Any relation to Earl?"

"No, he's the title of a poem by Edgar Lee Masters out of a book called *Spoon River Anthology*." I stood next to her.

"Okay." She crossed her arms and leaned back with a crooked smile.

"God, now I'm nervous. Let me see if can remember…"

Then I recited it to her as I'd done for my students to show them how it takes the human voice to infuse the words with a deeper meaning. Something Maya Angelou had said and I often used to get them to understand.

> *I HAVE studied many times*
> *The marble which was chiseled for me—*
> *A boat with a furled sail at rest in a harbor.*
> *In truth it pictures not my destination*
> *But my life.*
> *For love was offered me and I shrank from its disillusionment;*
> *Sorrow knocked at my door, but I was afraid;*
> *Ambition called to me, but I dreaded the chances.*
> *Yet all the while I hungered for meaning in my life.*
> *And now I know that we must lift the sail*
> *And catch the winds of destiny*
> *Wherever they drive the boat.*
> *To put meaning in one's life may end in madness,*
> *But life without meaning is the torture*
> *Of restlessness and vague desire—*
> *It is a boat longing for the sea and yet afraid.*

I stopped for a still moment, then recited it again for her. The second time, I slowed it down, especially toward the end.

"Wow, Carrie! That's impressive. I didn't know you had it in you. 'A boat longing for the sea and yet afraid.' Are you that boat?"

"I prefer a large truck," I laughed.

"A truck longing for the sea and yet afraid. I guess I should say so. That's an amazing poem. Maybe you can say it to me again sometime? Eh?" Malone said this, and put some fliers back in her mailbox.

"Malone, you haven't answered my question. Have you thought more about what I said? If it's no then just tell me. I can't stand the agony anymore."

"Look at you. You are a beautiful woman, Carrie. You can pretty much have any girl you want. You've got gray-blue eyes and white, even teeth and lips that are curvaceous and sultry and hair—" she reached out and touched my hair, "your hair is dark as black night and as soft as a linnet's wings, and your olive skin is so soft and..." She caressed my cheek with the back of her hand.

We stopped talking. Pregnant pause. Caesura. Blank page. She kept caressing my cheek and I enclosed my hand around her hand. I kissed her wrist. Then she pulled her arm away.

"Carrie, I am this goofy, preachy-teachy special ed. teacher who has been your best friend for a thousand years..."

"That's just it," I echoed. "A thousand years..."

"I am the queen of frumpdom."

"I like queens."

"Why now?"

"Why not?" I asked. I pulled closer to her and put my arm around her shoulders. "I don't want this weirdness between us. If you think it's too weird, then I will back off. Perhaps it is a phase. You know how we women like to go through phases." I managed a small giggle waiting for what should come next.

Then she exhaled while I held on to what I thought was going to happen.

Malone took a step backward. "I think I need some time to think about it. Can we just go back to being friends for a while? I think I feel more comfortable that way. Plus, you have your DUI day in court next month and you just got your Jeep back..."

"I saw the timbers by your house," I stated and then shifted back in my warm-up suit.

"Yeah, I'm going for the deck. I think our views might be similar onto that same vista outside of your backyard. I'm just lower." Malone crossed her arms.

133

"What do you think the school board is going to do?" I asked.

"You mean Jack, Carolyn and John? Well, John could care less. Jack is too formal but Carolyn is the swinger. If she votes that we should disband the GSA or whatever, we'll just have to try again next year."

"Why do you keep trying, Malone? Most people wouldn't do what you do."

"Then, that's the reason, don't you think?"

"Good point."

"If they squelch us, then I'm going to Lobby Day at the General Assembly to get some mic time to talk about what's happening here and why we need to get our legislators on the bandwagon to help our youth. I already have one organization called Mothers and Others who are going to help back me by being there."

Mumbling I said, "Voice to the voiceless."

"Stop mumbling. Let's get out of here and get some tea. I'm buying and don't even think about getting a beer or I'll pour it over your head."

"You can only pour it over my head if I say something stupid."


At the Stir Crazy coffee shop in the same strip mall near Ray's, Malone and I got Earl Grey decaffeinated tea. I thought I would throw up and she told me to get over myself. On the way over, I called Sammie and Charlotte. Sammie came driving in her produce truck and Charlote had just run eight miles getting ready for the marathon.

The coffee shop was winding down from a long day of espresso, steamed milk and the swiping of debit cards. How this country could still afford a five-dollar cup of joe, I did not know. Everything was closing. Pretty soon we'd all be riding horses to the grocery store for hay, horseshoes and assorted tack.

We four were all together and it felt simple and right and relaxing. Sammie in her butchdom sat down with a pack of cigarettes and everyone groaned. "Don't worry you bunch of losers, like, I'm not going to smoke." She struggled taking out a pair of tinsnips from her back pocket, a half-eaten carrot out of her front pocket, and then some rumpled up dollars and change to buy a beer and something to eat.

Charlotte's eyes bugged out. "Jesus, Sammie, you look like an ad for the Marlboro woman with the kitchen sink. All you need is a sponsor for Lowe's and your own produce shop and you may have an offer to do a cable show. What are these things?" She picked up the tinsnips and gazed at them.

Sammie laughed. "They get hair out of your nose, Charlotte."

"That's gross," Malone said, sipping her tea.

I looked at her but quickly averted my eyes to something else. My fingernails.

"Sammie, can you cut these?" I showed her my nails.

"I'll cut your hair," she said. She took a strand from the back and cut a small black chunk and threw it on the wooden table. "Going to open my own beauty parlor."

"I can't believe you just did that. Malone did you see that?" My mouth was agape.

Sammie laughed. "Here hand me your feet, Charlotte, and let me get ahold of those toenails that need some attention."

"Sammie," Charlotte half-screamed, "I think you've lost your mind!"

Sammie put the snips down. "I really do want to start my own salon. I'm sick of driving produce to Richmond every day."

Charlotte cocked her head to one side. "Sammie, since when did you get into beauty?"

"Like, clearly Charlotte, you haven't seen the clean lines of my own cut. I do it myself, you know."

"Yes," she said. "And, it looks like it."

"Don't care what you say. Am going to do it. No one can stop me. I've applied for the business loan. I'm like, forty-five years old. If I don't live my dream now, I never will. Can't do it when I'm eighty."

"Unfurl your sail, girl!" Malone said to Sammie. "Unfurl your sail. Go for it." Malone looked at all of us sternly.

"Yes, Sammie. Go for it!" I said. "You can do broccoli-do, the mushroom…"

"Carrie!" Malone interjected.

Charlotte laughed. "You can show people how to beet their hair into submission."

On that we all lost it. Even Malone. Sammie laughed and told us all to shut the hell up!

We did.

For a moment, we didn't say anything, and then Malone said, "Lettuce begin by saying that Sammie's dream is going to be fruitful."

Apoplexy settled in.

"You all just watch and see," Sammie said. "It will be better than you think and you're all gonna come running down wanting your hair cut, too, like!"

Charlotte was snorting. "Will you do like a Brazilian wax for me, or will you call it…or will you call it, or will you call it." She hit herself on the leg. "Will you call it peeling the potato." She hit me and Malone on the leg. We laughed but it wasn't as funny as Charlotte thought it was.

"Stick to running, Charlotte," Sammie said. "Go stalk someone."

Then we all lost it for the last time.

Sammie was a good sport.

# Chapter 14

In my rickety rundown Jeep, I sped with burps and grinds down Sterling Road to the high school the next morning. One week since my incarceration. My jail date was set for January. The road I drove was winding and bumpy in patches, a metaphor for my life, and it had a small pebbled brook running beside it. As I approached the school, I saw Malone outside with her special ed. students by the soccer field. Some were in small groups and some were hitting the ball around. It was early in the day to get started but that was how she did things. That was Malone. The students followed her and listened to her. Cichetti and Fortunata hung around with one another and I could see her giggling. For a moment, I thought I could see Fortunata mouth Elizabeth's name. Something to see for sure on my road of uncertain life. No, that couldn't be.

When I came into the front office, Snodgrass looked at me

and handed me the slip of crumpled paper. The referral on Tulio Grayson. "Tulio wasn't here last night, Ms. Tomlinson. He was with his dad out making hay. His father called me this a.m. to confirm."

"So, you're going to believe him over me on this?" I asked incredulously.

Then for the first time, I saw through the Snod. He didn't care. For a long time I hadn't cared either. That's where I'd been trapped. Then he said, "We need to drop this. There's not much I can do, especially when a parent vouches for a kid's whereabouts."

Grabbing the slip of paper from his weathered hand, I threw it in the trashcan. Piss on that I thought.

I scuttled over to Peggy Schindler and whispered that if Elizabeth Cichetti could only read the lunch menu, just the menu, nothing else, then could she come back. She said that if I got Snod's go-ahead then it would be okay with her.

Then I lied, "I'm sure he's okay with it."

"Okay then…but I'm not sure," she said, leaning over and looking in the direction of his office.

I dropped my leather portfolio on the counter and ran. I ran. I ran to the soccer field to get Cichetti. Getting something right for the first time in a long time. Go. Go. Go.

When I got there, I was out of breath and I couldn't find Cichetti or Fortunata. Lost. Hmm. Jesus. The day was chilly and I could feel the cool air in and out of my lungs as I breathily tried for someone, something. Scanning. The sun came into my eyes and then I spotted Malone.

"Malone!" I yelled half across the field. "Where's Elizabeth Cichetti?"

"She was just here…" She looked around.

"Malone, you lose her, too?" I laughed while darting my eyes in every direction. Malone came up to me in her frumpdom looking extra cute in a baseball cap and a whistle.

"You're so butch today, Malone."

"Shut up, you drunk criminal. Usually they sometimes go

down to the bench by the brook and sit. See if you can find them there. You'll like the literary allusion down there, I think."

"What?" I asked. "What are you talking about?"

"The best laid plans of mice and men..." She laughed and turned around.

Often go astray was the next part of that line.

I ran again. Go. Go...

This time I panted and heaved as I went down the hidden grassy knolled ridge to the brook where Cichetti and Fortunata were indeed sitting. The brook curved and swerved and there were rocks and stones that scattered in their own small circles and orbs. A mist like a fog emanated from the water in the brisk morning, and for the first time I felt separate from school and my ego and I experienced something spiritual there by the water with some of the dumbest yet smartest people around. No, just the smartest. There they were teaching me something about love I'd never seen.

I stepped closer, but then did not want to disturb what I saw. Cichetti was on her knees for what they must have acted out a thousand times. Perhaps she'd seen it on TV or read it in class. Her khaki pants were muddied at the knee and she had small rocks she had collected from the brook. Her tongue was hanging out as she arranged them in a circle on the bench.

Stealthily, I inched forward trying not to disturb them.

"Fortunata? Will you be my wife? Forever and ever and ever and ever..."

And then, Fortunata, pushed her hands in the air and laughed. Then Elizabeth laughed. I laughed.

Then I was outed.

"Mith Tomlinthon?" Cichetti stood up. Fortunata grabbed the small circle of rocks and shoved them in her pocket and slowly came up, too.

Stepping gently and closer, I stood behind the bench. "Whatcha guys up to?"

Fortunata's gappy smile filled her face and her crinkles were curvy and spectacular. She was beautiful. Then for the first time in a long while, she spoke. "M-m-m-arried." Both of her hands went into the air. Cichetti mocked her and did the same. Then I did it. We all three had our hands and arms in the air. For a moment, we made a circle and our arms and hands were in the air. It felt like heaven. For the first time, I knew where Susan was. For the first time, I knew where I was, too.

"Married!" I yelled. "Yeah, married!"

From the top of the hill, Malone yelled, "Come on you two lovebirds…we need to get back to the classroom in time for the announcements."

Oh, crap, that's right. Holy stupidity on my part. "Hey, Malone, I'm stealing Cichetti to get her to do the food announcements again. Schindler's okay with it as long as she doesn't start trying to marry off the whole school."

She waved back.

"Elizabeth?" I asked, calling her by her first name in a long while.

"Yeth. Mith Tomlinthon?"

"You feeling lucky today?"

She showed me her orange UVA band. "Yeth," she said with her swollen tongue.

"How about if we make a deal? Can you just do the announcements without asking Fort to marry you? I mean maybe you can make this bench and this brook your special place for that? You understand?"

Malone jogged toward us and piped in. "Elizabeth, honey, you just need to read the lunch menu. That's it."

"Yeth! Can Fort thit with me?"

Oh, brother, here she was the diplomat. Smart…so smart.

Malone looked at me. "Elizabeth, do you know what a compromise is?"

"No," she said, taking Fort's hand. Fort smiled again. I smiled back at Fort.

"Well, how about this. You do really well on the announcements for a few weeks and then we'll talk about Fort joining you."

I scrambled. "We have to hurry. I've gotten no approval on

this. But the sooner she does this, the better. I think it will help the whole school. I don't know why, but that's how I see it."

"Okay, Fort?" Cichetti asked her.

Fort nodded. And pulled out Flip and wound him up in her hand and giggled at the trick.

"Let's run Elizabeth. Pretend like you're on the basketball court."

We made it to the front office three minutes before the announcements were to be read. Schindler bit into her middle fingernail when she saw us walk through the door and then peered over into Snod's office. She cocked her head to one side. I sat Cichetti down next to her and Peggy softly read the lunch menu into Cichetti's ear. Cichetti smiled and breathed deeply and stared at the microphone. The microphone was her voice. It had been hers and the rest of us, too. I was just too dense to get it.

Peggy Schindler started. "Good morning, Sterling Road High School. Here are your announcements for Wednesday, November first. The tickets for our annual Thanksgiving Dance to be held the Saturday before Thanksgiving after the afternoon basketball game are now on sale during lunch. Tickets are six dollars per person or ten dollars per couple in advance. Ticket prices go up by two dollars at the door. Get them now, get them early. Gobble. Gobble. Principal Snodgrass wants you to know that rules will be read the week before the dance and that we will all adhere to the county code of conduct. A missing locket was found outside building six. If it's yours come to the lost and found and claim it. And, now, Elizabeth Cichetti will read the lunch menu."

Snodgrass peeled into the secretarial area and Cichetti grabbed the microphone.

"Good morning Thterling Road High Thchool," she read from the notes. "Today's lunch will be hamburger pattieth, french frieth and a fruit cup. Also, there will be grilled cheese thandwiches with cole slaw and a hot lunch of turkey, gravy and mashed potatoes. For dethert, there will be lemon cake and fruit.

Goodbye Thterling Road High Thchool. Thith is Elizabeth Cichetti."

She handed the mic over to Peggy and before she released the button, she asked me, "How was that Mith Tomlinthon?"

"Release the mic, Cichetti." I helped her.

Fine just fine, I thought.

Sterling Road High School did not have the blues the day—or in the ensuing days—that Elizabeth Cichetti read the lunch menu. Always in a good mood when she did it, and in each classroom you could feel the students and faculty have an internal smile each time she picked up the mic in the morning. It always seemed to set the tone for the day. Elizabeth Cichetti kept her promise.

For the entire month of November, my fifth period tried to finish the poetry recitations. Tulio Grayson, much to my dismay and pissiness, stayed in my class. He and his father evidently had the system worked out. Sammie told me that Tulio's dad worked on the side with Snodgrass and that it seemed the roots of loyalty ran deep among men. Tulio'd tried to stay the ultimate diplomat by trying to help the GSA, but Malone and I saw all of it falter after the hearing. He didn't care. He was just trying to be buddies with all the kids...now we were seeing through his contradictions.

"Sherry Proffitt?" I asked. "Are you ready to do your recitation today? If you can get through some of it, I will grade you accordingly. Right now, you have an F, but perhaps we can work that out. That goes for the rest of you. Are you ready, Sherry? Can we give this class some hope?"

The Gothic, heavyset, pimply-faced girl got up.

The class looked at her in shock. Jack Ignatio said, "Eeeeh."

"Jack, shut it!" I said.

He mumbled another, "E-e-e-e," but lower. I ignored it.

"Which poem are you going to do?" I asked. "Do you have a copy?"

With dirty fingernails and a cloud of dust that emanated

from her long, black jacket, she tenderly pulled out a crumpled poem and then slowly uncrumpled it as she walked toward me. A pungent odor decided to come with her.

Laying the poem on my desk, she ironed it with the back of her hand then stared at me.

I read from the title, "The Lake Isle of Innisfree" by William Butler Yeats. Ahem, you know that this is an Irish poet, right? This is an American literature assignment, Sherry."

Everyone laughed. Sherry kept a straight face. I was shocked, nonplussed. When the laughing was over, she shrugged and said, "My sister is at the Charlottesville Home. This poem is the first thing I see every time I go in there. I feel like that makes it American."

What could I say? "Okay, Sherry, "The Lake Isle of Innisfree." Whenever you're ready."

Slowly, she sauntered to the front of the room like she had some sort of Gothic terminal illness. For the first time all semester, the entire class was silent, even the repulsive Tulio Grayson.

"If you need a prompt, just nod your head and I'll give you one."

She stood behind my podium and grabbed it. For a second I thought she might drive the podium right out the door.

She spoke so low and quietly that we all had to lean in to hear her.

"*I will arise and go now, and go to Innis—go to Innisfree…*" she stumbled. I had the lines in front of me in case she needed help. She went on to the next line, "*And a small cabin build there, of clay and wattles made:…*" She stopped, looked up, then looked down. A small enow was heard from the back of the room and I turned and glared at the perp.

She went on. "*Nine bean-rows will I have there, a hive for the honey-bee, And live alone in the bee-loud glade.*" She smiled. I nodded. Good. Then like a ray of light came into the room, even though it was raining, she did the rest of the poem without any hitches or glitches at all.

"*And I shall have some peace there, for peace comes dropping slow,*

*Dropping from the veils of the mourning to where the cricket sings;*
*There midnight's all a glimmer, and noon a purple glow, I will arise*
*and go now, for always night and day I hear lake water lapping with low*
*sounds by the shore; While I stand on the roadway, or on the pavements*
*grey, I hear it in the deep heart's core."*

I stood and clapped while the others stood and clapped. The most glorious moment of our fall in fifth period. There were a few whistles and some enows. Clearly, they didn't know what the hell enow meant. I asked the thin girl next to me, Roxanne Wright, what it meant. She shrugged. "It's some dumb hip-hop word. No one knows what it means. That's the beauty of it."

"Sherry," I said. "What do you think that poem means?"

"I don't know," she said. "I just like it. It makes me feel like home or something. Home, I guess."

"Good. Good for you, Sherry. I'm proud of you. How long has your sister been at the Charlottesville Home if you don't mind me asking?"

"Her whole life. My parents can't afford to take care of her, so she stays there. We visit on the weekends."

"Oh, I see." And that was exactly it. I was beginning to see.

# Chapter 15

"Malone, calm the fuck down, I can't understand a word you are saying." I jumped up from my cracked leather couch and held the phone eight feet from my face. It was the Sunday after the big Thanksgiving Dance and Malone was dithering this and dithering that, unable to talk in complete sentences.

"Why didn't you stay at the dance, Carrie?" came the phrase.

"I was tired. We lost to Lunenburg by twenty points, I wasn't in the mood to celebrate." I ambled into the kitchen and got a glass of water then listened to her intently as I wiped down my counter with a musty rag.

"Well, Snodgrass got on his portable microphone and told everyone at the dance that there would be no bumping and grinding and no lewd and lascivious behavior which included same-sex dancing. Every GSA kid including Thunder Bucknell did it anyway and then all of them hovered around Elizabeth and

Melissa and let them dance with each other."

"Well, that's good isn't it? Like the circle of light. Sort of like our day by the bench. Cute."

"Carrie, will you please listen?"

"I'm trying, Malone."

"Snodgrass called the Cichettis and the Fortunatas to come and pick them up and then Nate Fortunata said he would be to the school on Monday to withdraw Melissa from classes."

"And take her where?"

"I'm not done."

"What?"

"Elizabeth ran away. I got a call from Annie Cichetti this morning thinking I could help find her."

"And?"

"Well, I'm calling you, dumbass!"

"Malone, don't call me dumbass or I'll put you in a grave."

"Then put me in a grave, Carrie. I'm worried. Elizabeth takes medicine and she doesn't know where she is. And she doesn't know where she is. *And she doesn't know where she is!*"

"Malone. Do you know how many times I've lost her at practice and at games? I think she has a good idea as to where she is."

"School?"

"Possibly. I'm getting dressed. I'll pick you up in twenty minutes."

"Carrie?"

I fumbled with my pants. "What?"

"Carrie, will you call Sammie and Charlotte? I know they can help, too."

"I'm on it. We need a good stalker and truck driver who can produce something."

Thirty minutes later, Sammie picked me up and then Malone and Charlotte in her big produce truck. We could sit up high and scan the streets of Charlottesville and run by the high school in case Cichetti was there. Poor girl. I wouldn't be surprised if she'd taken the bus to the Radio Shack in Charlottesville to buy a mic.

"Let's start at the high school and see if she's milling about," I suggested.

"Good idea, Carrie." Malone said this and put her hand on my leg. It was the first act of intimacy she had shown me.

My blood caught fire in a split second and a chill ran down the back of my neck, slowly, gradually. Looking at Charlotte who saw the same, she winked at me and shook her head to one side intimating I should hold Malone's hand. I did. I curled my veiny hand around Malone's and she gripped mine back. For the first time, our bodies came together in a nervous, perhaps lusty kind of way: at least I was hoping.

Malone returned to the real world with a plea. "Turn around, Sammie and go back to my house. We need to get River. She knows what Elizabeth smells like and is a certified Delta dog. Most places will be okay with her coming in and sniffing around, at least let's hope so."

Sammie did a twenty-point turn in the large produce truck and we fruits went back to get River.

Malone released my hand, hopped out of the truck and ran all the way inside to get her, shouting, "Come on, girl!" River came out wagging and Malone put on a special bandanna and collar around her. "This is going to be your first unofficial job."

Bounding to the truck, River jumped in back. Good girl. She was a Shepherd Lab mix and her slobber-o-meter was up to full flappy speed by the time we got to the first stoplight.

When we heard sirens, River wailed and we all put our hands to our ears.

Exasperated that it was taking too long to get to Sterling Road High School, Malone yelled, "Can't we get this truck to go any faster?"

"Malone, like, settle your crack down. We're getting there as fast as we can," Sammie barked back and ground out the gears and released the clutch too early. Accidentally, the truck turned off. The tension was almost seeable in the air.

"That's it. Let River and me out. We're walking!" Malone yelled.

Sammie cranked the keys. It was a ruh-ruhr, and then it started again.

"Malone, you're making us all nervous. Elizabeth Cichetti is okay. We will find her," I said.

"Are you sure?"

"I'm sure." I reached for her hand and River slobbered over my right shoulder.

She grabbed my hand and this seemed to settle everyone down. Women.

Sammie pulled into Sterling Road High School and we all made a break for the four different areas of the school. Charlotte headed for the cafeteria and the buildings around it; Sammie went to Malone's classroom and to mine; Malone went to the gym with River; I went to the soccer field to the bench. We were to meet up in twenty minutes for a full report of what we would find or not find.

It was a gloomy Sunday, and I trekked across the soccer field in my hoodie and jeans. My boots crunched the November grass and I made a beeline to where I thought Elizabeth might be: at the bench. When I came over the hill: nothing, no one. An empty bench. I was crestfallen. My wish was visceral to see her there as I'd seen her recently with her toothy grin, her orange wristband, her khaki pants and white Oxford shirt a size too big.

Then I went down to the curvaceous brook and thought of Sherry Proffitt's poem and how peace comes dropping slow. I skittered a rock to the one side of the brook and then reached into the cool water to find a stone. When I pulled the rock from the brook, I had a heart stone: a rock, ragged on the sides but shaped just like a heart. Yes, peace does come dropping slow. For gay people, especially, I thought.

When would this resistance ever end? When would our day come, Martin Luther King? You got any answers? When will our day come, Jesus Christ? I flung the rock across the brook and then lost my footing and fell right into the water. My head was totally submerged. Fuck. I had banged my head against a rock and then I heard laughing. Not from Sammie, or Charlotte or Malone—but from Melissa Fortunata. She was on the other side of the brook just up and back out of my initial viewpoint.

"Fort...Fortunata...Melissa?" I asked. "Hey, help me up out of here!"

Ever so gently and sweetly, like every step counted, Melissa Fortunata broke the water's surface and came my way. She reached out a hand, giggled, and then helped pull me up.

"Thank you!" We held hands as we crossed the brook to the other side.

"Welcome." It was one of the ten words she could say.

"Fortunata? What are you doing here?" she shrugged. "Do you know where Cichetti is? We can't find her?"

"She don't know where she is. And, that's fine with me and Gwen here."

In his flannel and oxygen tank, Nate and Gwendolyn Fortunata were on the opposite side of the bank. Just up the tree-lined hill were a bunch of low-income house apartments and trailers.

Nate spoke again, more heavily than before. "We're going to take her out on Monday. We've applied to the Charlottesville Home and they are accepting her. It's too much for us. I'm sick and Gwen here works near around the clock. No one is here to take care of her."

Gwendolyn, who was wearing dirty jeans and a sweater and a red scarf, said, "We can't do no more. She won't go to the bathroom by herself unless I keep watch. I got two shifts. Melissa's been peeing behind the trailer. People been talkin'. It ain't right what those boys did to her. We can't handle this school no more and Nate is too sick while I'm gone to keep an eye on her. The Charlottesville Home is nice. My nurse friends collected some money to help with the fee."

I was wet along the side of my head and there was some blood on my temple. Wiping it clean, I said, "I think that's a good idea but what about Elizabeth Cichetti? Have you thought what this might do to her?"

Nate stepped forward, angrily. "Now you listen here. That

Eddie Cichetti is some big real estate guy and he can get and do whatever he wants with his money and his family. I've got to look out for my own. That Elizabeth can visit Melissa in the Charlottesville Home if she wants but that's all. That's it. Melissa has been, what is the word, traumatized. Is that right Gwen?"

Gwen nodded.

He continued. "She's been traumatized and we want her safe. In a safe place. A place where people can look out for her. That Malone woman has done a good job but this last thing with those redneck boys...enough is enough."

Amen and an enow to that I thought.

"Carrie, Carrie, Carrie!" Malone was screaming and running down the bumpy ridge with a slight gimp in her giddyup. "We found her. We found Cichetti—or rather, River found her." She waved and continued the bumble downward.

"Hey, Melissa," Malone said as she jumped across the brook. "Heard there was quite a lot of fun at the dance the other night. You okay today?"

"Yes." Fortunata ground out the word in a torpor. We all hung on the yes.

In a bit of irony, I grabbed Malone's hand and looked at her intently. "Where did you find her? Or, where did River find her?"

"By the boys' bathroom, sitting against the door playing with her frog. River has licked every bit of food off her face from last night and this morning. I think it was ketchup and eggs and something saucy."

Then from over the hill came Cichetti. River was hopping next to her and Cichetti's shirt was all the way out of her pants.

"What happened to your head?" Malone wiped the blood that was continuing to ooze from my temple. The brook's water was cold—I was cold. "How come you're wet?"

"Just giving Fortunata a show on how much fun it is to slip and fall in the brook," I said and then reached over and muffed Fort's hair.

River bounded through the brook, and like it was a match made in heaven, she trotted directly and easily over to Fortunata. Licking her face and whining, she head-butted her on the side and Fortunata patted her head and squatted down to her. River jumped up and put her paws on her shoulders and licked her right in the mouth. Fortunata put her arms around her and hugged her as if she'd found the friend she'd always been looking for. Cichetti sidled up to the both of them and frumped down on the wet ground.

Sammie and Charlotte came to the ridge and exhaled and then quickly sat on the bench.

"Call the Cichettis," I said to Malone.

"I will. Just give me a minute."

The Cichettis came and picked Elizabeth up and Eddie and Nate and Gwen and Annie all shook hands and it seemed to be okay. Parents of special students knew a humility that no other parents on earth did. It was a conundrum and enigma how they bore out their days. But, they did. The love that special children emanated was the reward for the humiliation, the frustration, and the tolerance of the day in and day out life that would never end. Even if they placed Fortunata in the Charlottesville Home—her being would never ever be gone. Neither would Cichetti's.

The GSA was disbanded on Monday by Snodgrass and a large vote by Carolyn from the school board. It was too much trouble and the community was getting up in arms. Everything needed a big fat squelch—twist the cap tight on it.

Fortunata was easily placed in the Charlottesville Home. It was a grand place overlooking a park and a lake where geese waddled about and dog owners took laps on the sidewalk. Five stories high, it held over two hundred residents with mental and physical disabilities. The building was all brick and had a circular drive for access for vans that took residents out into the world each day.

Elizabeth Cichetti wanted River and Malone to visit Fortunata every night. Malone did the best she could. When I didn't have a game, I took River with me and Cichetti (when Annie and Eddie allowed) and we visited. It soon became clear that Fortunata looked forward to our visits because it was the only time she felt safe going to the bathroom—when River went with her.

On the weekends, Malone and I went together and always took River. My disaster of a basketball season ended and the holidays came and went like holidays sometimes do. If I ate one more ham biscuit and tried to pretend like I was enjoying the fa la la's, then I was just kidding myself.

Then something weird began to happen and I couldn't put my finger on it.

On the last of Christmas vacation, Malone and I visited the Charlottesville Home and Cichetti and Fortunata were lying on the bed together: sweet. Just hanging out playing with old stones and Flip. River jumped on the bed and lay down at their feet. Cichetti and Fort giggled when River started licking Fort's foot. The home smelled like Christmas with scented candles burning and dinner wafting smells of onions and potatoes and turkey down the hall.

"Melissa," Malone said. "I'm not sure if you are going to understand this or not? But, I'm doing my best."

Cichetti looked at Malone. "You're lucky, Mith Malone!" Then she looked at me. "You're lucky, Mith Tomlinthon!" And she smiled with her tongue half out like she always did.

"River is going to stay with you from now on, Melissa. I'm giving her to you for keeps. Okay? That way you can go to the bathroom and she'll keep you safe. You won't have to go behind the building anymore. Okay?"

Fortunata, at first, did not seem to understand. But, after a minute, she got up and took River into the bathroom and shut the door. That was it.

Fortunata just needed a companion.

Sometimes that's all that anyone needs.

I was stunned at Malone's gift. I was stunned at her mercy. I was stunned period.

# Chapter 16

Prior to the closing of the 2009 General Assembly session in Richmond, Audra Malone was fired up, prickly fired up like someone was stoking her from behind. Of course, all I had to do was take a personal day and go watch her speak in front of the General Assembly at Lobby Day. Recently, whenever she asked me to do things, I showed up. A first for me.

She asked the Cichettis if Elizabeth could go with us like it was a field trip and, much to our surprise, Annie said yes. Eddie was out of town. Annie wrote an excuse for Elizabeth for the school and we were on our way for the hour drive to the state's capital.

Cichetti asked sixteen billion times if we could go see Fortunata and River at the Charlottesville Home. I told her yes and that we would visit and get ice cream and go see Fortunata and take them both to a UVA basketball game after it was all said and done. Every fifteen minutes I repeated the same speech. Finally I said, "It'll all be for luck, Cichetti."

When I said this she smiled and twiddled her arms in the air. I twiddled mine back and she laughed hysterically. We all rode up front together in my rickety Jeep. Cichetti in the middle. Down Interstate 64 we sailed.

"Carrie, keep your hands on the wheel!" Malone looked over her speech while I drove. Her nerves were virtually glowing outside of her face and neck.

"They're on the wheel—see?" I put my hands in the air. "It's going to be okay. We'll be sitting right next to you," I said.

"We could lose our jobs over this, you know," she said, pinched like a prune.

"Who's going to see us? You get up, say your five-minute speech and then we ride home. Simple as that. We'll be lucky! Right Cichetti?"

"Luck. It's for luck, Mith Malone!" Cichetti threw her head back and laughed.

"I don't think it's going to be that simple, Carrie." She put her hand on my leg. Cichetti saw this and put her hand on my leg, too.

"You guys are dense," I said.

"You're dense, Mith Tomlinthon! We going to get popcorn tonight at the game?"

"Yes."

"Are we going to get french frieth?" she asked. "You need a bracelet, Mith Malone."

"Yes, we will get fries."

"Malone?" I asked.

"Yes."

"Are you nervous?"

"Of course I'm nervous. I stayed up all weekend preparing this speech that the entire House and Senate will hear. Any one of them can ask me a question, I think. But, I only have, like, five minutes. That's it, five minutes to change some social thinking with you, the insular basketball coach, with Cichetti, our Down

Syndrome example, and me, the one with the panic attacks."

"You get panic attacks?" I asked.

"Yes, and I sweat all over like some kind of farm animal and my neck breaks into what looks like a flashing beacon."

The drive did not take long—a straight shot on I-64 to Richmond in an hour and fifteen. Malone and I agreed that we'd look for Sammie's train wreck as something cool to do prior to our chat on state Capitol Hill.

Once in Richmond's historic district where Jefferson had made his historic speech to separate church and state and nearing the state capitol, we drove to the bottom of old Church Hill. I peered around at everything Sammie had told me about to find that capped train wreck of 1926. After explaining to Cichetti what to look for, she leaned over me to search herself. Malone made notes on a legal pad and I, for once, noted the grandeur of the city juxtaposed to the poverty we drove through. There were old tenant homes that were so rundown ivy was growing through the brick and into the exposed living areas. African American men walked along the sidewalk with blank stares. I saw two women of the night, and evidently the day, hanging out by a street lamp looking just as blank as the society in which they lived. Hopelessville.

"There it is!" Crunching through a Cheeto, Elizabeth saw it first.

"Slow down for a second," Malone said. "Let's take a look."

Right next to Richmond Cold Storage—Sammie was right. There was a large tunnel opening capped off with overgrown brush and ivy.

"We've got a few minutes. Let's take a quick look…"

"I don't know. Maybe we should get to the capitol. I really need to get my bearings before my beacon starts to go off."

"Let'th look." Elizabeth had the door halfway open, clambering over Malone.

I pressed hard on the brakes thinking I might lose Cichetti to the concrete. We all got out and Cichetti brought her bag of munchies. Just over the concrete walk that was overgrown with cold dead weeds, there was a small deck that led into Richmond Cold Storage: evidently the place where Sammie left and picked up produce. We all three ambled precariously up the steps and then down the steps into a small field of defunct overgrown grass and weeds and poison ivy. Because of the cold, most everything had taken on a brown tinge. The trees were scary looking and they sheltered the opening so it was hard to see it from the short distance to the road.

Without talking, all three of us moved through creepy-ville. Every now and again, I heard Elizabeth crunch on a Cheeto. Thirty seconds into the walk and just a bit around an old oak tree, the gigantic capped archway appeared to us. Up against the hill, the grandiosity made me hold my breath and I grabbed Cichettti's hand.

"Jesus Christ!" Malone said. "Can you imagine?"

We paused. We reflected. We pondered.

"No. They're all entombed in there from what Sammie says," I remarked, letting go of Cichetti's hand and moving closer to the capped tunnel.

"What are you talking about?" Elizabeth asked.

Malone never lied to her students. "Elizabeth, a very long time ago—see where it says 1926 stamped on the concrete?"

Elizabeth nodded. "Yeth," and she shoved a Cheeto in her mouth mesmerized by Malone.

Malone continued, "Well, there was a train wreck in there and the people who were in the train never got out."

"Why?" Cichetti asked.

I then reached out and gently touched the concrete. "Because if they had tried to get them out of there, then the people trying to help would have gotten hurt, too. Or worse, they would have died."

"Tho, they are thtill in there?" Elizabeth asked.

"Yes, they are still in there," I said, washing my hand over the large tombstone.

"Thtuck," Elizabeth said.

"Stuck," Malone repeated back.

156

"Like I'm thtuck in here?" Elizabeth said and pointed to her temple. "I'm thtuck in here, right Mith Malone?"

Elizabeth Cichetti had made the best analogy I'd heard in years. I could drink ten beers, write about metaphors and similes, and express my love on a legal pad but never come up with an analogy like that. In her inherent Down Syndrome wisdom, she knew she was different from everyone else. I did not know she knew. I thought all people who were stuck in their heads through mental retardation, mental illness, physical malady were all dumb to the paralysis they were in. But, she was not.

I looked up. Malone was crying. She turned around and walked back to my Jeep Cherokee about to make the biggest speech of her life to help not only the Down Syndrome adult with us but the kids at our school whose voice had been squelched by the school board. She had five minutes to change the thinking of the House and Senate. But, if she was the woman I was in love with, she could do it. Shifts and changes in thinking sometimes just took seconds, minutes.

After the train wreck, I never looked at anyone with a mental or physical handicap the same.

I stopped being stupid.

When we arrived on Capitol Hill, Elizabeth had to pee. The grandeur of the building was nineteenth century: Doric columns lined the entryway and there was a smell of old history emanating from the walls to the frescoed ceilings. The bathroom was just as ostentatious as the rest of the building, daunting, almost ominous with its flowered wallpaper and gold inlaid carpeting that had roses and all kinds of fretwork and meandering. We both went with her to do the same. The bathroom theme coming up again. This time I felt relatively safe on state Capitol Hill, much more so than Sterling Road High School.

And then it happened.

"Carrie? I can't do it." Malone pulled me to the side as we entered the bathroom. "I can't go out there and make a speech that anyone will listen to. Can you do it for me?"

"Holy guacamole, Malone. I don't even know what you're going to say."

We were standing by the mirror. Malone's neck was starting to take a bit of a fiery look.

"Just raise your collar up, Malone, and you can do this."

"I'm panicking." She walked to the window. "I need some air." She rolled the old window open and I sidled up next to her.

"Malone." I put my hand on her shoulder. "You're going to be fine. Just breathe."

"That's the problem. I forget to breathe. I have a panic disorder, Carrie. I know this is important and all but I need your help. Can you support me just this once? How many times have I been there to support you?" Then she started to cry.

Elizabeth swung the door open from her stall and exclaimed, "I'll help, Mith Malone! Don't cry Mith Malone. I'll help."

"For crying out loud, Malone. Give me your notes. Let me see your notes."

Malone rifled through her bag and then sat down on the floor. A voice appeared in the doorway. For a second, I thought of Tulio Grayson. "Four minutes till assembly reconvenes. Four minutes..." came the voice.

"Hurry, Mith Malone." Elizabeth egged her on.

She pulled them out. "Here, here, here they are!" Her face was flushed and beads of sweat streamed down her face. We all stood up from our huddle.

I calmly said, "Put your face in front of the window and feel the breeze. It will cool you off for a minute."

Then, from the corner of my eye, I saw a spider's web on the inside of the bathroom window and a moth, a small moth was trapped inside of it. From deep within my heart's core, I reached up and carefully pulled the moth from just within the spider's reach and freed it. Malone had done it for me months earlier when I was afraid, too.

"Malone?" I asked. "You feel better?"

"Yes."

"Then let's go!"

Once inside Assembly Hall it looked a lot like Congress. There were people all around who were helping people find their section and then asked about your time on the mic and that the delegates and senators would listen to you for five minutes and take into account the nature of your question or problem or whatever. When we took our seats, Elizabeth was the first to notice the microphone in the middle of the walkway. In a fit of hilarity she pointed at it and then looked at Malone and me like it was the eighth wonder of the world. Of course, to her, it was.

I thought I might have to call an ambulance for Malone but once she settled into the fact that I was going to give the speech for her, her neck began to deflate.

I whispered to her, "It's going to be okay. Stop fidgeting and get a grip on yourself. Hang on to Elizabeth so she doesn't try to get to the mic before me." I tried to make her laugh but she just smiled as if she were still in the throes of a panic attack.

Reading through Malone's notes, I wasn't sure I could actually follow them. She had statistics and testimonials and diagrams and heliograms and all sorts of things that did not make sense to me. For fifteen minutes, I tried to get a grip on what exactly her point was but couldn't find it. It was same-sex dancing, the marriage amendment, the GSA rules and regulations, health care, welfare, histrionics, food stamps, Down Syndrome having the right to marry if they want to. It went on and on and I couldn't prioritize the importance of any of it. Then, when I asked her a question, she just rolled her eyes and pointed at her watch.

Delegate Cantor spoke in his microphone and Cichetti had a little jiggle. I rested my arm on hers and noticed she had a menu from SRHS that she was evidently studying for the next week.

"Next up," he said, "we will be listening to some testimony from Albemarle County about county taxes. We have a Mr. Ed Snyder who will be discussing the need for some extra funds for his county and three others as well. Then we will listen to some testimony from Audra Malone on the need for GSA privileges in her county as well as a proposed resolution to bring in legislation that will end the Marriage Amendment passed in 2006. I warn you now that we may only have time for one of your discussions. After that, we will recess for lunch."

"Lunch!" Elizabeth screamed it.

The entire assembly turned to her.

"It's okay," I said to everyone and no one. "She likes lunch. Loves to eat." Then I got nervous.

Ed Snyder got up to the microphone and droned on and on about the situation of the roads, especially up toward Hadleysburg and how we needed more money to reduce the number of potholes. He even had pictures of potholes in Nelson County, Greene County and parts of Albemarle. Most of the delegates of the assembly paid no nevermind to what he had to say. He was a gray-haired farmer and wanted to try and do something about the thing that bugged him the most.

After what seemed like an eternity, Cichetti was snoring in her seat and Malone just kept checking and rechecking her watch. I was continuing to fumble through the papers when Delegate Marsh asked me to step to the podium.

I got up and dropped the legal pad papers and Elizabeth popped up. She helped me pick up the papers and then followed me to the microphone. She held a piece of my black pants for security as she watched all the eyes roll from her onto me. Her shirt was untucked and so was mine.

A blaring noise came from the mic as I got too close and then I tapped it. "Ahem, my name is Carrie Tomlinson and I'm employed by Albemarle public schools; specifically Sterling Road High School. We're know as the Blues...go Blues," I said, then Elizabeth echoed the same sentiment. My voice echoed in the chamber and the pages and people milling about listened with little regard. The faceless people in skirts and suits peered through me. Some chatted, some looked at notes, some stared blankly.

"What we are here for today is to have a moment to argue two points. One is the allowance of a GSA, that is a Gay-Straight Alliance, to form, and the other is to repeal the Constitutional

Amendment that bans same-sex marriage."

"Uh, Ms. Tomlinson, you can only speak to one of these matters at a time; pick the one you think is most important to your faculty and students." Delegate Marsh looked down his nose at me. Which one? Which one? GSA? Marriage? Which one?

Collective giggling and laughter on the floor. I paused. Elizabeth tugged on my pants. "Not now, Elizabeth…"

Then it hit me like I'd been asleep for two thousand years.

"First," I continued. "The Virginia Constitution was amended three years ago when it did not need to be amended. It did not need to be amended to protect the religious sacrament of marriage. Churches, temples and mosques have never been, and could never be, required to recognize marriages that are not in line with their faith traditions. Such action would violate Virginia's Bill of Rights founded on Jefferson's Statute of Religious Freedom and the First Amendment to the United States Constitution. But I think the members of Equality Virginia covered this…" I fumbled for some more information. I glanced at Delegate Marsh—a large luminous black man, listening.

"Secondly, there is no case pending or any other valid reason to think that how the Constitution is today is absolutely necessary to protect the sanctity of civil marriage in Virginia. Virginia law already prohibited same-sex marriage, civil unions and more *before* the amendment was passed. In the year before the amendment, this body voted for a law that also prohibits any 'other arrangement' that purports to bestow any of the benefits or rights of marriage.

"We have enshrined this prohibition of same-sex marriage in the Virginia Constitution. We have done what other states have done: we have constitutionalized discrimination. Let me repeat: we have constitutionalized discrimination.

"Far from merely protecting traditional marriage, constitutional measures passed in other states are already being applied to justify discrimination against gay men and lesbians that goes far beyond prohibiting same-sex marriage."

I turned to Malone and mouthed, this is good!

"Uh, Ms. Tomlinson, your time is almost up," Delegate Marsh stated.

"Mith Tomlinthon?" Elizabeth was tugging at my pants again. "Can I go now?"

The assembly exploded in laughter.

"Wait one more minute," I said. "In addition, in Michigan, passage of a marriage amendment has been read to require the state to end a popular program extending health care benefits to the partners and children of state employees, leaving hundreds, if not thousands, of taxpaying Michigan residents and their dependents without access to health insurance coverage.

"In Ohio, the passage of a marriage amendment, including language not unlike the language of the amendment offered here, has already led criminal defense attorneys to argue that the Ohio Constitution now protects their gay and lesbian clients from domestic violence charges.

"One can only guess what additional arguments lawyers will invent to use the proposed amendment as a rationale to strip away the few protections Virginia citizens have against discrimination and violence based on sexual orientation. One of the ones we want to continue in Albemarle County is that of the student-led GSA. Students there need a voice.

"The Virginia Constitution should never, again, be amended to single out a group for disparate treatment. Virginia's painful history of mandated segregation, disenfranchisement of black voters and prohibitions on interracial marriage have left an indelible stain on Virginia. We need not add another.

"Virginia should not take the radical step of codifying in Virginia's Constitution discrimination against hundreds of thousands of taxpaying Virginians. We need our children to take measures starting today to get our legislature back."

Before I could finish, Elizabeth pulled the mic to her and spoke. "Good morning, Mr. General Athembly," she said. "If you come to Thterling Road High Thchool this week we are having spaghetti on Monday and turkey and mashed potatoes on Tuesday. Then, if you come, you can see where my girl lives: Fortunata.

She lives in the Charlottesville Home. She's going to marry me. You'll see. She likes me. Goodbye for now Mr. Athembly."

The delegation stood and clapped. I didn't need to say a thing. If I could have given Elizabeth the mic sooner, she would have said it all.

"Uh, well, this is nice and all, Ms. Tomlinson," Mr. Marsh said. "But I really don't think a, excuse me, retarded girl and a nice clipped speech will be your ticket to changing the laws of Virginia, now do you?"

"We're having fudgies, too," I said. "They taste the same whether you're married or not."

Everyone laughed and we left.

I held Malone's hand all the way back to Charlottesville.

Two days later, I lost my license to drive anywhere for a year except school and Alcohol Substance Abuse Program meetings. It all happened in Greene County court. Malone sat quietly in the pews and watched.

# Chapter 17

Three months later it was spring. Spring meant baseball, softball and a general slowing down of the enow's in my fifth-period class. Tulio Grayson was suspended for fighting half the time and my basketball team was doing off-season weightlifting, which usually meant I had to oversee it in some regard. Pickle complained that her weights were too heavy and Juanita Jones continued to smack her on the butt with a towel. I stayed away from Principal Snodgrass as he'd allowed the GSA to disband, allowed Tulio Grayson to stick around, and gave both me and Malone an unpaid personal day after he'd heard about our special trip to the General Assembly through Vickie's father who worked for two of the senators in the House in Richmond.

Cichetti continued to read the lunch menu in her Cichetti way and for the first time in months, the school seemed to settle a bit, its own fissure healing. The GSAers gave up till the next school year and Thunder Bucknell said he didn't care because he was graduating anyway. No one ever listened. Why should people start now? He didn't care. Exactly how I'd felt for most of my life. Most of the other kids just did their own thing. Many of them on occasion traveled to Richmond where there was an organization that supported gay youth. Rural areas were the hardest hit; at least metro Richmond had a larger outreach.

Malone and I remained friendly even though I longed to be with her, to touch her, just to be intimate. She said she needed me to show her that I was serious about not drinking and serious about staying single for a period of time. She was killing me with the wait as my attraction intensified over cups of tea, trips to the Charlottesville Home, and how she managed to be everything I wasn't. Twice in the faculty lounge I caught her looking at me, furtive glances. Each time, I returned with a faint nod beginning to know that the attraction was growing between us as the wait, the anticipation to be near her shrunk.

On the Tuesday before graduation, we had a surprise visitor from the House of Delegates in Richmond. Snodgrass escorted him to the cafeteria where Malone and I sat eating cheese pizza and telling kids to throw away their trash.

As the group walked in, I wasn't sure who he was at first, but he was clipped, prim and proper and his suit was so tight I thought he might burst out of it. It was Delegate Marsh. Snodass looking impressed as hell, introduced us to him.

"I hear you have really good fudgies here," he said, shaking our hands.

Malone and I both stood up.

"Why, yes," she said. "They are really good. Can I get you one?"

Snodass interrupted. "Delegate Marsh is here to talk about your trip to the General Assembly back in January." He looked at us strangely. "I didn't realize you had taken Elizabeth Cichetti…"

Malone had traipsed off for the fudgie and left me standing

there. "Yes, Malone and I and Elizabeth had quite the time on our Lobby Day Field Trip."

Delegate Marsh's voice was deep. "These ladies made a fine speech and even Elizabeth had something to say."

"Yes, she read the lunch menu," I laughed.

Snodass clearly didn't think this was very funny.

Malone came back with a fudgie and handed it to Delegate Marsh.

He peeled the wrapper off and began to eat it. "Hmm. This is good," he said. "Well," he said through bites. "You are all probably wondering why I am here. First of all, you can't pass up a good fudgie. Second of all, I've gotten together with my constituents and we've decided to introduce a few things next year in the 2010 Assembly. One is the repealing of the state's constitutional marriage amendment. Now, don't get me wrong. This may take years. But, at least we have to make a start. The second is the right for GSA's to form from the point of view of the sponsor and school needs. In other words, it should be sponsor-driven and school-driven and the codes of conduct statewide need to support them and the rights that they want and deserve."

Malone about lost her dentures.

"Mr. Marsh," I asked. "Why this, why now?"

He finished his fudgie and then tossed it twenty feet into the nearest trashcan and made it. "Because, you see, when I was a boy, we grew up in the projects and my mother and father always told me that love was love. It had no ethnicity, race, creed, religion, sexual orientation, nor mental illness nor mental incapacity. Your young Down Syndrome girl taught us all that. We've been talking about it since you all were there. I was hard on you. I'm sorry."

"So, you've come all this way to tell us that?" I asked in disbelief.

"You came all the way to the General Assembly to make your speech?" He asked.

"Yeah."

"Then enough said." He smiled and patted me and Malone on the back at the same time.

"Enow!" I yelled and put my arms in the air.

Everyone looked at me funny but I didn't care. Six of my fifth-period inmates including Sherry Proffitt stood up and did the same: "Enow!"

Enow was enow.

# Chapter 18

Sammie came over to my house the Friday night before graduation and we made virgin mojitos. Charlotte brought the mint and we cut out makeshift tombstones for the grass near my swing under the oak. Charlotte painted my name on one and Sammie painted Malone's name on another. I hadn't had a drink in three months and it sucked.

Sammie began to argue with me. "Do you really think this is, like, going to woo Malone into kissing you?"

"Shut up, Sammie, hurry—she's going to be here in thirty minutes and I have to get these tombstones outside and planted in the grass." I ran around my clean kitchen, rewiping the counters down.

"Carrie, this is a little morbid. Maybe you can just take her to the movies or something?" Charlotte crossed her eyes and put her hands on her hips.

I yelled. "And kiss her there? Are you kidding? There's no privacy at all! Malone will get this. It's right out of Spoon River where all the poems are written on tombstones. The people and the story of their lives. It's about death and transformation. Death is transformation—not an end. A life's story doesn't end at death. Sometimes death is the beginning."

"Hurry up and get the hell out of here, Sammie. If she sees that big produce truck, she'll know something is up! I've been planning this ever since I wooed her in the front office when I recited that poem to her. I'm like Earl Grey—unfurling my sail."

Charlotte interjected, "Like what's the price of celery?"

"Oh, you're such the consummate stalker!" Sammie irked out at her.

"When do you open your hair salon, Sammie?" I asked.

Charlotte and Sammie both halted.

"What?" I asked, and stopped in my tracks then pulled up my khaki shorts.

"We're both verklempt," Charlotte said and reached out to hold Sammie's hand. "You actually asked about Sammie. For the first time in your life, Carrie, you've asked about someone else. Let us pray." They put their heads down.

"Shut up!" I yelled.

All three of us laughed and bumbled down the side of the hill and planted the fake tombstones next to the tree near the swing.

"Do you have your poem?" Charlotte asked.

"Yes," I said. "Now you guys have to go. You think they look okay?"

"The tombstones?" Sammie asked. "They look bizarre, especially if you're finally going to make a move on her. Jesus."

"Christ," Charlotte finished.

"Shut up, you two! Malone will understand. It's between her and me! Now go, get out of here, thanks!"

Sammie and Charlotte drove off, no doubt to go to Ray's—a place I hadn't been to in several months.

I yelled thank you and they both simultaneously bowed

their heads again. I gave them both the finger and then tucked in my blue T-shirt. Then I slammed the door and put my hands through my hair.

Twenty minutes later, Malone showed up.

I was nervous. She came in and threw down her bag on the leather bench by the door. Her cargo shorts were cinched around her waist with a leather belt and she had on a sleeveless red button-down shirt. Her lip gloss shimmered and her eyes looked still, sober, and soft.

I walked out of the kitchen. "Hey, come on in. I've got some virgin mojitos for you and me."

"Virgin?"

"You know me, Malone. I love a virgin—mojito I mean. Been on the wagon now for a while you know."

"I'm proud of you, Carrie. That's something. Ever since the General Assembly and the DUI conviction, you've gotten your act together. Even the kids on your team seem to be working better after your losing season." She picked up a mojito and saluted me.

"They are in postseason, but you're right. They seem to be doing all right. Can't wait for intramural play this summer." I poured myself a mojito over the sink. Malone came up from behind me.

"What are you doing Malone?" I asked.

"Do you know how many dishes I've washed here looking at these stones and that picture of Susan?"

"A billion."

"Correct."

"I've got something to show you, Malone, but we need to go outside. You can still see since it's twilight."

"Okay, but I need to say something to you, Carrie. I need to read something to you."

"Okay," I said. "But can you do it outside?"

"Yes."

With mojitos in tow, we walked out onto the deck and just beyond the oak tree where the old tree swing was my makeshift cemetery.

"What is all this?" Malone asked.

"Remember that poem I read to you from *Spoon River Anthology* a long while ago when you spoke for the first time in front of the school board? The one about George Gray? Remember: we were in the office and I recited it to you—twice?"

"Carrie, this is a little morbid. Don't you think?" She walked down to the white gravestone markers we'd dug into the ground, the ones with my name and hers on them. "Jesus, Carrie, I'm not dead yet. And, for that matter, neither are you!"

"I know, I know. I'm just trying to make a point."

"Well then, Carrie, why don't you, for once, shut up and let me make a point instead. Come sit down here on the grass with me." She put her mojito down and I sat down next to her.

"I've written you something," she went on. "So, you're just going to have to let me say it. I know you are the poet but I've been working on this for quite a while. Can you listen?"

"Yes." I swallowed hard and sat cross-legged from her behind my own grave marker; she sat behind hers.

"I'm embarrassed." Then her neck got red.

I put my hand on her leg and said, "Malone, it's just me. I've been the one pining for you for all these months while you've stayed rather silent. So speak the hell up. I'm ready!"

"Okay, here goes. Don't laugh or I'll leave." She retrieved a piece of paper from her pocket and unfolded it.

"I promise I won't laugh."

"I wrote this for you," she said gently.

She began:

*Notes From Your Windowsill*


*In your kitchen on the windowsill*
*Rocks and hearts of stone and glass lay delicate on*
*The brown, grainy wood—an altar*
*I hear words when I wash dishes like*

*"God grant me the serenity…"*

"Stop," I said. "There isn't a stone that says that on my windowsill."

"Shut up," Malone said. "I put one there recently. Are you going to listen?"

I nodded.

*Then of course, "Grace," whispers melodic melancholy*
*To where "healing" resounds under*
*The red-stoned ring I left with you*
*Months ago…the circle of my adoration for you,*
*Lusty on its precipice of love.*
*Next, a golden angel and a white, sandy heart of clay*
*where Scout's paw is its lasting impression*
*her walk of life eternal here and, of course, showing*
*An altar's purpose—love.*

*At your kitchen window,*
*I wash the millionth dish of the day.*
*And silently say hello to Susan and want to ask Emmanuel*
*Where is she hiding? Where has she been?*
*The windowsill says, "She's right here."*
*I pour water on the soap and stare at the old yellow roses*
*Your father cut for you, finally—*
*At your kitchen window, I see outside an ancient swing*
*I want to push you on when there is no time—just us.*
*Through the looking glass of your kitchen window,*
*At your kitchen window, one day, I save that moth from the spider's*
*web.*
*"Strength" from the window's sill—"Save it!" I did for you, my*
*love.*

*At your kitchen window, I have drifted up from behind you*
*when you were the dishwasher and windowsill watcher,*
*and longed to wrap and enfold my arms about you,*

172

*head on your shoulder to see what you see;*
*We are framed then, you know—two of us in the looking glass,*
*Much like a picture or a portrait*
*Our altar beneath us;*
*I want to hold you like the sill holds the meaning you have put*
*there.*

*I want to love you as playful as the swing might sail in the wind of*
*your life*
*As horses rest and eat in the pasture of heaven;*
*I want to kiss your neck and whisper the poetry of love and life into*
*the chambered nautilus and keep it there...*
*always with the kind of pressure and desire you want—*
*much like the longing cadence of your heartbeat when you first*
*wanted me in*
*June of the year we were to meet and I was to come*
*and make love to you and*
*wash your dishes and learn about*
*life's love and meaning and purpose through your windowsill.*

I said softly when she was done, "Malone, it is June."

"Carrie, it is June."

"You left me that red-stoned ring. I wondered where that came from?"

I knocked over my gravestone as I moved toward her. Unhurriedly, I thought. It is Malone, so, unhurriedly. Like a chalice, I cupped her cheeks in my hands and let the energy build between us, slow, letting the daggers of our life fall about us and take in the stillness supposed to be there. I didn't have the right poem for the woman before me. She did. Malone the poet.

We kissed on the grass all night till our lips were tight and chapped and our tongues were numb from exploring the humanness of each other; the secret senses of each other. She unfurled my mouth; I unfurled hers...we were no boats; just two women seeking what wanted to be sought in the melancholy of a June night. We rolled in and onto each other and my legs intertwined into hers, and hers into mine. We became root systems, pushing and prodding. My arms went around her and hers around me and the rocking of our bodies and the soul oil that passed between us was fiery and lusty and true. I whispered in her ear, "More," and she said, "Yes," in mine. When Malone said, "Yes," I pressed more, feeling the hole in my soul fill with the love I pushed out with my tongue and the love she pushed in with hers. With our clothes on, we made new words for love that had no font, no pitch, no letters, no syllables: just the beating of two hearts pounding together, making marriage a different word, a sanctity with no rules, no churches, no walls—just truth.

Sometimes even that word wasn't strong enough. But, I was no wordsMith Just a woman in love with my girl. My gratefulness was for her ability to wait for a stupid, retarded self-serving English teacher like me.


The next night was graduation, and we all lined up in our college colors and walked out onto the football field where Elizabeth Cichetti with her almond eyes looked up and asked me if I had an orange UVA wristband. Did I have a flippy frog in my pocket?

After I gave her over to Malone, Malone came over to me and had a large grin on her face.

"You can't be smiling from last night?" I laughed at her.

She blushed, "Well, yes. But more so, Elizabeth just asked if she could read off some of the names for graduation. She's been eyeing her frog and the mic since we got everyone in line."

"Did you hear her yell to Fortunata?" I asked, adjusting my sunglasses to the setting sun.

"No. She did?" Malone asked. She was sexy, Malone, now in her robe and school colors.

"Yes. She's over there with River. You see her?" I pointed to the stands and raised my sunglasses.

Malone scanned the bleachers. "Oh, yes. She loves that dog. I barely get to see her except on weekends now."

"Maybe we can get a puppy? I've let Scout go enough now that I think it's time." I patted my heart.

"You've let go of a lot of things, now haven't you?" Malone said, sliding her hand down to touch mine. I quickly grabbed her hand and held her with my eyes.

I blushed, momentarily thinking of Susan. "Yes."

We walked together in procession to watch Elizabeth Cichetti graduate into life. When she received her diploma, she put her hands in the air and yelled out, "Mith Tomlinthon! Mith Malone! Fortunata! The names in that order. We collectively put our hands in the air, too, like signaling a touchdown but better. The first rite of passage Cichetti would take this summer.

The second rite or right of passage she would take on August sixteenth when she would marry the love of her life: Melissa Fortunata. River would assist Fort down the aisle with wedding rings pinned to her collar. River would sit patiently, wagging her tail while Malone and I sat in the front row holding hands—witnesses to a love with no rules.

Laws can take years to change. Ancient laws. Years and years.

But, with two special girls from Sterling Road High School in Charlottesville, Virginia and a decent mic—we can begin now.

Like Yeats, I hear it in the deep heart's core.

Windows open and a voice to the voiceless.

**Publications from
Bella Books, Inc.**
*The best in contemporary lesbian fiction*

**P.O. Box 10543, Tallahassee, FL 32302
Phone: 800-729-4992
www.bellabooks.com**

WARMING TREND by Karin Kallmaker. Everybody was convinced she had committed a shocking academic theft, so Anidyr Bycall ran a long, long way. Going back to her beloved Alaskan home, and the coldness in Eve Cambra's eyes isn't going to be easy. $14.95

WRONG TURNS by Jackie Calhoun. Callie Callahan's latest wrong turn turns out well. She meets Vicki Brownwell. Sparks would fly if only Meg Klein would leave them alone! $14.95

SMALL PACKAGES by KG MacGregor. With Lily away from home, Anna Kaklis is alone with her worst nightmare: a toddler. Book Three of the Shaken Series. $14.95

FAMILY AFFAIR by Saxon Bennett. An oops at the gynecologist has Chase Banter finally trying to grow up. She has nine whole months to pull it off. $14.95

DELUSIONAL by Terri Breneman. In her search for a killer, Toni Barston discovers that sometimes everything is exactly the way it seems, and then it gets worse. $14.95

COMFORTABLE DISTANCE by Kenna White. Summer on Puget Sound ought to be relaxing for Dana Robbins, but Dr. Jamie Hughes is far too close for comfort. $14.95

ROOT OF PASSION by Ann Roberts. Grace Owens knows a fake when she sees it, and the potion her best friend promises will fix her love life is a fake. But what if she wishes it weren't? $14.95

KEILE'S CHANCE by Dillon Watson. A routine day in the park turns into the chance of a lifetime, if Keile Griffen can find the courage to risk it all for a pair of big brown eyes. $14.95

SEA LEGS by KG MacGregor. Kelly is happy to help Natalie make Didi jealous, sure, it's all pretend. Maybe. Even the captain doesn't know where this comic cruise will end. $14.95

TOASTED by Josie Gordon. Mayhem erupts when a culinary road show stops in tiny Middelburg, and for some reason everyone thinks Lonnie Squires ought to fix it. Follow-up to Lammy mystery winner *Whacked*. $14.95

NO RULES OF ENGAGEMENT by Tracey Richardson. A war zone attraction is of no use to Major Logan Sharp. She can't wait for Jillian Knight to go back to the other side of the world. $14.95

A SMALL SACRIFICE by Ellen Hart. A harmless reunion of friends is anything but, and Cordelia Thorn calls friend Jane Lawless with a desperate plea for help. Lammy winner for Best Mystery. Number 5 in this award-winning series. $14.95

FAINT PRAISE by Ellen Hart. When a famous TV personality leaps to his death, Jane Lawless agrees to help a friend with inquiries, drawing the attention of a ruthless killer. Number 6 in this award-winning series. $14.95

STEPPING STONE by Karin Kallmaker. Selena Ryan's heart was shredded by an actress, and she swears she will never, ever be involved with one again. $14.95

THE SCORPION by Gerri Hill. Cold cases are what make reporter Marty Edwards tick. When her latest proves to be far from cold, she still doesn't want Detective Kristen Bailey babysitting her, not even when she has to run for her life. $14.95

YOURS FOR THE ASKING by Kenna White. Lauren Roberts is tired of being the steady, reliable one. When Gaylin Hart blows into her life, she decides to act, only to find once again that her younger sister wants the same woman. $14.95

SONGS WITHOUT WORDS by Robbi McCoy. Harper Sheridan's runaway niece turns up in the one place least expected and Harper confronts the woman from the summer that has shaped her entire life since. $14.95

PHOTOGRAPHS OF CLAUDIA by KG MacGregor. To photographer Leo Westcott models are light and shadow realized on film. Until Claudia. $14.95

MILES TO GO by Amy Dawson Robertson. Rennie Vogel has finally earned a spot at CT3. All too soon she finds herself abandoned behind enemy lines, miles from safety and forced to do the one thing she never has before: trust another woman. $14.95

TWO WEEKS IN AUGUST by Nat Burns. Her return to Chincoteague Island is a delight to Nina Christie until she gets her dose of Hazy Duncan's renown ill-humor. She's not going to let it bother her, though. $14.95